PRAISE FOR CARLIE ST. GEORGE

Carlie St. George's stories take you on a journey through anger, hurt, sorrow, and hope. They're unsettling and hauntingly beautiful and speak of truths hidden just beneath the surface, daring you to look, asking you to understand. Carlie is a fantastic writer and *You Fed Us To the Roses* is unforgettable.

—DAMIEN ANGELICA WALTERS,
AUTHOR OF *THE DEAD GIRLS CLUB*
AND *CRY YOUR WAY HOME*

You Fed Us To the Roses is a book that presses Scream Queens against Riverdale and says "now bite!" A dizzying journey through a world you will recognize, populated by people you've likely met—because they are you, and me, and all of us. A treat, a nightmare.

—E. CATHERINE TOBLER, AUTHOR OF
THE NEBULA-NOMINATED *THE
NECESSITY OF STARS*

D1188598

Carlie is an author with a unique vision of the world and a master at treading the line between the heartfelt and the chilling. In *You Fed Us To the Roses*, you will find characters full of humanity and a need for connection in a world that makes less sense than a cult slasher film. Dying is not the end of the world here. Losing the ones you care about might be.

—EUGENIA TRIANTAFYLLOU, AUTHOR OF *THE GIANTS OF THE VIOLET SEA*

Carlie St. George has written a collection that speaks in the voice of an older girl who's going to take you to a place you're not supposed to be and let you in on stories you're just a little too young to hear. You'll die petrified and grateful.

—MEG ELLISON, AUTHOR OF *NUMBER ONE FAN*

No one turns a trope inside out like Carlie St. George. *You Fed Us to the Roses* offers humor, horror, tenderness, and trauma in one sharply beautiful package.

—JULIA RIOS, EDITOR OF WORLDS OF POSSIBILITY

Carlie St. George has one of the most distinctive voices in horror today. Every story in this sharp toothed collection is different, but united by St. George's unique blend of terrifying, incisive, and heartrending while somehow also managing to be extremely fun. *You Fed Us To The Roses* is an exciting, frightening spike of adrenaline into some of horror's oldest tropes that will surprise and transfix even longtime horror fans.

—LEIGH HARLEN, AUTHOR OF *BLOOD LIKE GARNETS*

An intoxicating, haunted trip into fairy tales painted bloody. I didn't want it to end, and each story was more devastatingly lovely than the last. Carlie St. George is a forever must read for me now.

—KRISTI DEMEESTER, AUTHOR OF *SUCH A PRETTY SMILE*, *BENEATH*, AND *EVERYTHING THAT'S UNDERNEATH*

Simultaneously sharp, self-aware, and intensely affecting horror writing. This collection displays an impressive range of imagination and unease, heart and gore. Highly recommended.

—PREMEE MOHAMED, NEBULA AWARD-WINNING AUTHOR OF *AND WHAT CAN WE OFFER YOU TONIGHT*

You Fed Us To the Roses is the perfect short story collection for my horror film loving heart. Carlie St. George gives us slashers, queer final girls, urban legends and ghosts re-imagined, in a compelling, nuanced voice that had me scared, smiling and guessing what could come next. I loved it.

SUZAN PALUMBO, AUTHOR OF THE NEBULA AND SMALL PRESS AWARD NOMINATED SHORT STORY "LAUGHTER AMONG THE TREES"

YOU FED US TO THE ROSES

SHORT STORIES

CARLIE ST. GEORGE

ROBOT DINOSAUR PRESS

Robot Dinosaur Press

www.robotdinosaurpress.com

(Robot Dinosaur Press is an imprint of Chipped Cup Collective)

YOU FED US TO THE ROSES: Short Stories

Copyright © 2022 by Carlie St. George

All rights reserved.

No part of this book may be reproduced in any form or by any electronic or mechanical means, including information storage and retrieval systems, without written permission from the author, except for the use of brief quotations in a book review.

This is a work of fiction. Names, characters, places, and incidents either are the product of the author's imagination or are used fictitiously. Any resemblance to actual persons, living or dead, events, or locales is entirely coincidental.

ISBN: 978-1-949936-47-6 (ebook)

ISBN: 978-1-949936-48-3 (paperback)

ISBN: 978-1-949936-49-0 (hardcover)

Introduction © 2022 by Wendy Wagner

Cover artwork © 2022 by Evangeline Gallagher

https://www.evangelinegallagher.com

Interior design by Bog Wolf Cover Designs

Edited by Merc Fenn Wolfmoor

For Papa,

*I miss you. I wish you were here to see this, and to gently chide
me about all the profanity that lies within.*

CONTENTS

YOU
FED US
TO THE
ROSES

CONTENT NOTES

You Fed Us To the Roses is a collection of dark fantasy and horror short stories, many of which deal with disturbing subject matter and themes. For the book as a whole, the following list includes overarching content warnings.

- ableist language
- animal death
- bullying
- child death
- domestic violence
- gore
- harm to animals
- intimate partner abuse
- murder
- parental death
- parental neglect
- physical abuse

- religious abuse
- sexual abuse
- suicidal thoughts
- suicide
- violence (combat, slashers/serial killers)

While we have done our best to include TWs on each story, unfortunately no list will cover everything that may be potentially harmful to every reader. If there are specific content elements you would like to be informed about prior to reading, please send an email to info@robotdinosaurpress and I will attempt to answer as promptly as I can. Thank you.

—Merc Fenn Wolfmoor, editor

INTRODUCTION

WENDY N. WAGNER

What can I say to ease your journey into the world of Carlie St. George? If this were a fairy tale, I would be the mysterious hooded figure standing beside the path leading into a dark forest, and you would have to choose whether to step into the weeds to talk to me, hoping I might offer a boon of wisdom—or else to run past as quickly as possible, fixing your eyes on the deeper darkness ahead.

Choose wisely, dear reader. Your heart is on the line.

I was lucky enough to read Carlie's work as it came out, beginning in 2016 when we worked together editing her story "Every Day Is the Full Moon." After that exposure, I made sure not to miss a single piece. But I got to take the slow and sunlit path through her work, experiencing these stories over the course of several years as magazine after magazine released them. You are about to plunge head-first into a realm of magic and pain, beauty and trauma, loneliness and love. I can't guarantee that you won't find yourself changed by the experience, your heart alternately broken, crushed, healed, restored, and, ultimately, doubled in size.

I must warn you that many of the stories in this collection draw on fairy tales, dipping into that ancestral stockpile of uncomfortable wisdom and updating it for our contemporary era. Stories like "Monsters Never Love You" (reworking both "The Juniper Tree" and "Hansel and Gretel") and "Such Lovely Teeth, Such Big Teeth" (a modern epilogue to "Little Red Riding Hood") explicitly reference fairy tale characters and plots, while stories like "You Were Once Wild Here" and "Every Day Is the Full Moon" are original fiction that draw on the symbols and themes of fairy tales. Like fairy tales, these stories use the power dream logic to speak the truth about situations we tell ourselves are inescapable and to expose truths about ourselves we'd prefer hidden.

Every fairy tale is set against the backdrop of the dark and dangerous forest—but the truth is that the forest might be safer than the homes the characters were forced to leave. In a Carlie St. George story, home can be a difficult place. The stories in this collection feature complicated families and abusive parents. They showcase families with secrets and families who don't understand. Like the heroes in fairy tale, the protagonists of these stories must find their own paths through the forest. Sometimes their parents meet them at the end, their relationships improved by the night in the woods. And sometimes, the protagonists must find new families to treasure them.

That journey to belonging is part of what makes these stories so powerful. These are all stories about girls who are outsiders and misfits. Most of the protagonists are gay or ace or otherwise queer. They're faced with the terrible choice to squash their authentic selves into a neater package or to grow into themselves, no matter how strange or monstrous they might become.

Don't get me wrong: this book is about monsters. That's because it's about girls, and society is terrified that girls with power will become monstrous. To protect itself, society has created an enormous quantity of stories to instruct and warn girls into behaving "properly." Consider the slasher flick and the urban legend. Don't these stories reward the good girls and punish the bad? Don't the witches in fairy tales always come to a bad end? This book attacks those tropes. Whether the stories in this book are speaking to fairy tales, or slasher movies (like the stories "If We Survive the Night" and "Some Kind of Blood-Soaked Future"), or urban legends (like "Three May Keep a Secret" and "Forward, Victoria"), they challenge and undermine society's stories about controlling girls' behavior—the stories that try to keep girls from becoming the kinds of free and powerful women who can remake the world.

I can feel you hesitating, dear reader. From the nervous expression on your face, I know you are thinking that you, too, would like to remake this world of heartbreak and difficulty. In that case, I can offer you a piece of wisdom I learned reading Carlie St. George: We don't need magic to make it through the dark forest. We just need bold hearts, and truth, and the power of a few true and loving friends.

Take my hand and we'll walk together along the forest path. These stories, dark as they are, will light our way.

—Wendy N. Wagner
   October 2022

SOME KIND OF BLOOD-SOAKED FUTURE

SOME KIND OF BLOOD-SOAKED FUTURE

HERE'S THE THING about surviving a slumber party massacre: no one really wants you around anymore[1]. All your friends are dead, and your mom is dead, and you get shuffled off to live with your miserable Aunt Katherine, who blames you for getting her sister killed because she's an awful human being like that. And you try to move on, but you don't know how because your nightmares are constant and therapy is hard, especially when a new killer arrives and murders your therapist with his own pencil. You survive that massacre, too—this one's on a field trip—but nobody cares that you saved some band kid's life because, clearly, you're cursed and should just leave town. Even the band kid isn't grateful, that pimpled little shit.

So, you leave town. But first, you rob your aunt blind.

---

1. Violence, harm to animals, ableist language, underage drinking, suicidal thoughts.

Here's the thing about leaving town: you start getting scared everyone's right.

You're living in your car, which at first is pretty fun, right up until you realize you don't have a diploma or a GED, and your entire work history is three months at a shitty diner, a job you still had to have a home address and three personal references to even apply for. Also, it's four in the morning and you really have to pee, but it's pouring and you're alone, parked on some dark road near a forest full of howling things. Your only choices are either to brave the storm or finish the bottle of Gatorade and awkwardly squat over it in your backseat; you try the latter and end up with a mess, which means your car now smells like pee, which means your home now smells like pee, and you just want to give up, drive home, and admit defeat. Aunt Katherine would never take you back, though; you'd probably enter the foster system and get some abusive church lady, or, worse, somebody wonderful, someone who doesn't know how to cook and earnestly fails at slang and lets you cry on her shoulder whenever you wake up screaming. And a month will pass, then two, and you'll think *it's over, it's okay, we're safe*, until one day you come downstairs to find New Mom at the table, an axe in the back of her head and blood pouring out of her mouth and into her cereal.

You can't let that happen to another mother. You can't let anyone else die because of you, which means this is it; this is your future: alone, in a smelly car, until you run out of money and die. No. You have to do something. You have to make a plan. A five-year-plan, just like in school, only cross out applying for scholarships or taking the SAT's. Replace them with…replace them with…

You can only think of the things you stole from Aunt Katherine, especially the gun.

But you're not ready. You're so scared. You fought so fucking hard to live.

Eventually, you fall asleep. In the morning, you drive to a new town. Buy an air freshener. Drink some coffee. Spot a flier for tonight's frat party. Your dead friends would've loved a party like that, would've begged you to sneak in with them. Peer pressure isn't really your problem anymore, though, so instead you drive south for hours. You only hear the news days later: FRAT HOUSE MASSACRE, 14 DEAD.

It's terrible. It's a tragedy. It's evidence you aren't to blame, that there's slaughter in this world that doesn't solely belong to you. You didn't talk to any of these dead guys. You aren't responsible for any of this—

But you can't stop thinking about that band kid.

Jesus, what an asshole. What a typical Nice Guy turd, and you could've let him die, but you didn't, and there's *power* in that. Maybe you'd have saved more people, if you'd gone to that party. Maybe if you came across the killer yourself…

Well. You're not going to find out anything sitting here.

You drive back and it might be suicidal, but at least it's suicidal in an active way? That sounds suspiciously unhealthy, but you're too busy to consider it further: the frat's sister house is planning a memorial kegger because nobody ever learns anything, because the definition of insanity is who the hell knows, but the definition of *willful ignorance* is doing the same thing over and over and expecting different results. Whatever. The important thing is, you smell bad, so you sneak in a shower at some public gym before heading over to the sorority house. Can you pass for eighteen? Nope. But everyone's drunk, so they let you in anyway.

You try to find the killer before any of the girls die. It doesn't work: one gets smothered with her own sorority flag, while another is chopped in half mid keg stand. But you do shoot the killer right in his creepy doll face before a freshman gets disemboweled. Well. Okay. She gets a *little* disemboweled, but she's still alive when the paramedics come, and that means she'll be okay, probably. Anyway, that's still a dozen girls without a scratch on them. All psychologically scarred, sure, but there are limits to what you can fix.

One of the drunk girls hides you until the cops leave, and there, under the bed, next to a bunch of dirty clothes and—gross—a used condom, you think, *well, it's a reason, anyway. It's some kind of blood-soaked future.*

Altruism isn't putting gas in your car, though, so you make that drunk girl give you a hundred dollars and some fancy Juicy Couture shit to replace your gory jeans.

Here's the thing about your new future: it's hard and it's sad, but mostly it works.

You drive from town to town, looking for signs. Wild

parties. Incompetent sheriffs. Fatal pranks one-to-five years prior. It gets easier to spot them. Easier to spot the girls, too, the ones killers gravitate towards: nice girls, good grades. Virgins, all of them.

You used to have good grades. Used to be nice, too.

Virginity, though, is still your superpower. It doesn't keep you alive, but it improves your chances. It means you can kill the monster, or die trying. It means you die last. It means you find the bodies.

Most people find that sort of thing traumatic, though, so you try and help them avoid it. Find the impending massacre. Track down the virgin. Get them the fuck out of town and slay the monster in their stead.

It's not a career for everyone. It's hard on the clothes, and you can never have sex. But honestly, that last part's a bonus, because you're ace as fuck, and it's really rewarding how your sexuality comes with practical benefits like this. Doesn't pay great, though. Some can't afford much, even when they're grateful. Others are just assholes you have to persuade with your gun. Your mom would be pretty horrified; she didn't believe in violence, so that axe to the head must've been an especially big shock. But you need that money: for gas and tampons and laundromats and weapons. Food, too, although there's not always much left for that. You almost get killed once by some asshole in a Dobby mask—a *Dobby mask*—because you haven't eaten in two days and get dizzy when you try to stab him in the balls.

You make friends with this kid, José. You try not to make friends, but it happens sometimes: not all research can be done from the library, and you have to infiltrate the school: walk around, pretend you're a new student, duck whenever a vice principal walks your way. You interrogate José for gossip because he looks sharp. He secretly follows you back to your car because, well, you weren't wrong.

José tries to help you save virgin Zoe and the entire Valentine's Day Court. The King and Queen are lost causes, but everyone else would've been fine if the bucktoothed sheriff hadn't bust in and arrested you for vagrancy, among other things. Considering you were holding a hacksaw at the time, you're lucky he didn't just shoot you. Still, by the time José breaks you out, the killer has resurrected and killed the sheriff, two deputies, Zoe's boyfriend, and Zoe's mom.

You decapitate the killer. It doesn't feel like a win. You have an overwhelming urge to get so drunk you can't even see straight. That's sure what José does. You force him to drink water, get him into bed. He grabs your hand when you reach for the light.

Stay, he slurs into his pillow. *Please.*

You shush him gently, tell him he's okay, but he shakes his head and almost rolls off the bed. *YOU*, he says loudly, pointing. *Don't go. You're not. Don't…*

No one's ever asked you to stay before. Maybe you cry a little, but he's too drunk to notice.

It's not safe to stay, though, and anyway, he's wrong; you're doing fine.

Here's the thing about never sticking around: the towns all blur into one another until one day, about ten months after you ran away, you're back in California. You end up in this two-stoplight town where a gravedigger somehow impaled himself on his own shovel, but that was just an unfortunate accident, and those missing teenagers? Playing hooky, obviously. Can't be anything more than that: this isn't the big city, after all.

You find the virgin almost immediately. Actually, she finds you: Joey Santiago, seventeen, named after Josephine Baker and Joey Guerrero, and, she tells you confidentially, Joey Potter, too. You're not sure what to do with that information since you don't know who any of those people are, but she's already handing you a water bottle as you put your last five bucks in the tank. Apparently, Joey and her mom foster a houseful of rescue dogs, and you're the human equivalent of a sad, hungry puppy with a broken tail. She insists you come home for dinner.

Mrs. Norwood is a pretty Black woman in her late thirties: tall, muscular, very short blonde hair. She delicately asks if you'd like to use the shower, and finds you absurdly long pink pajamas to wear, and loads up your plate with more take-out than you've ever seen. *Don't worry about the cost, honey*, she says. *Just eat up, and maybe we can discuss your living situation tomorrow.*

You desperately want to go along with it. These people are so kind, and you're so tired, and these empanadas are so fucking good you're about to cry…but you can't risk it. Mrs. Norwood is Black, and Joey is Black and Filipina, and all PoC, but especially Asian people, are way more likely to die in these scenarios, virgins or not. Not to mention they live in a converted barn with bad cell reception and six dogs, and the only reason the killer isn't already here is that Joey's half-sisters live an hour away with their dad. There just aren't enough victims for a proper slaughterhouse.

So, you give it to them straight and wait for the inevitable questions about your sanity. Instead, Mrs. Norwood takes her daughter's hand and says, *in this house, we believe in masked killers. Global warming, too.* And Joey's trembling, but her eyes are focused. *Will he leave me alone if I'm not a virgin? Because that's a social construct anyway, and my boyfriend lives five minutes away.* And Mrs. Norwood makes a face, but that doesn't stop her from asking *will that work? Because I do have condoms,* and you vow to yourself, here and now, that you will protect these precious people at all costs.

Unfortunately, that's when the doorbell rings and six teenage girls pile in with presents and a Safeway birthday cake. Joey's surprise party is supposed to be tomorrow, but one girl has to babysit and another has some cheerleading competition, and before Mrs. Norwood can make them leave, the lights cut out, and a dog, barking loudly, suddenly goes quiet. *It's too late,* you say. *He's here.*

Two girls immediately assume it's a prank. You tell them they're wrong, and they say shitty things about you and mental asylums. Joey goes off, which is delightful but also poorly timed, as it distracts you from stopping the panicked cheerleader from running out the door. By the time Mrs. Norwood calms everyone down, it's clear the party isn't going anywhere: every car has a severed fuel line and the cheerleader has a severed head.

Everyone screams a lot.

You get them all back inside. That includes the dogs, even the little black one who's definitely losing that leg but, shockingly, isn't dead yet. It's been a while since you could afford bullets, but you gather every knife in the house, all except the kitchen shears, which have mysteriously gone missing. Then you gather the girls in the living room, trying to make it to dawn.

You make it fifty-seven minutes, just enough time for two pieces of birthday cake and a ton of high school gossip: Madison, the blonde who was an asshole to you, used to date Joey's boyfriend. Charlotte, the brunette who was an asshole to you, hates Sam for beating her in girls' javelin. Sam, the only other brown girl, thinks Emma's basic; also, a slut. Emma, who wears both terms proudly, might be cool if she didn't constantly say things like *I don't mean to be racist, but*. And the babysitter, well. You don't even know her name, since she hasn't spoken since the cheerleader died. Joey's efforts to comfort her go pretty well until Emma, completely ignoring everything you've said, gets too close to a window. She's quickly impaled through the gut, her body pulled outside.

The babysitter half-faints. You seal up the window, but now someone else is screaming: a guy, somewhere out back. Charlotte says it's her boyfriend, Jake, or maybe Joey's boyfriend, Tyler; they were both going to sneak over with beer after Mrs. Norwood went to bed. *We have to help them,*

Charlotte insists, and runs out the back door into the dark. There's a strange, gurgling sound. Then, nothing.

Soon, someone emerges from the fog.

It's Tyler. *They're dead*, he says, bleeding from a non-vital place. *Oh God, oh God, they're dead.* You want to kill him right now, but no one else will let you. They won't even let you tie him up, an obviously reasonable concession, probably because he insinuates you're crazy and lesbian-obsessed with Joey. Madison apparently believes in homicidal lesbians so much that she actually attacks you; you twist her arms behind her and yell, *Joey, why are you friends with these horrible people?*

No one has a good answer to that, but Sam does ask where Tyler's car is. Tyler doesn't think it matters. *The killer probably cut my fuel line, too*, he says, but that only makes Joey back up. *We never told you about the cars*, she says, and Tyler's all *whoops* before he pulls Madison from you and stabs her in the face.

This time, it's not just the girls screaming; Tyler does too because he's one of *those* types, maniacally laughing as he slashes forward like a drunk Robin Hood. You don't bother dodging much, just slide a boning knife straight into his heart.

Oh, Tyler mouths, and dies.

So. Easy.

Mrs. Norwood hugs Joey, and Sam hugs the babysitter, and you just stand there, looking at your left arm. It hurts like a motherfucker—Tyler cut it up pretty good—but there's only minimal blood on your pants and shirt.

Too. Easy.

It's not over, you say but Mrs. Norwood doesn't hear you, opens the back door. *I'll check on the others*, she says, and you scream—

But someone's already stabbed her with the kitchen shears.

The killer is tall and narrow, wearing a dark robe and a devil mask. Mrs. Norwood collapses at their feet, while Joey screams and Sam turns and runs. The killer breaks a nearby broom across the countertop and launches it forward. It spears through Sam's chest into the front door. She slumps over, half-hanging and dead.

You look back at Mrs. Norwood. For just a second, you can't move. For just a second, you're not even in this house at all.

But then she gets up.

Her skin is ashy, her forehead beaded with sweat. The shears are still embedded in her shoulder. But she's on her feet, and when Devil Mask stalks past, Mrs. Norwood tackles them into the dining room. Immediately, she collapses again, but it's enough to snap your brain back into action. You kick Devil Mask in the devil mask; they grab a chair and knock you into the living room. Something squelches unpleasantly underneath you. You think of a body exploding into blood and cream, but of course it's just Joey's half-eaten birthday cake.

Hands around your neck, then. You reach for something, anything. You can't breathe. You can't—but your fingers grasp something, even as you knock away the mask.

Of course. Asshole brunette. Girls javelin. Ran outside to "check" on her boyfriend.

Fuck you, Charlotte, you wheeze and stab the plastic cake fork in her eye.

Charlotte screams and reels back. She pulls an actual goddamn machete, but Joey kicks her in the head soccer style. The machete flies up in the air.

Still coughing, you catch it and shove it right through Charlotte's fucking lying mouth.

Now. Now you're covered in enough blood for it to be over.

It hurts to move. You do it anyway, staggering over to Charlotte's purse as inexplicable sirens wail nearby. Charlotte has ten bucks, which isn't enough to repair your car by a long shot. Tyler doesn't have any cash at all.

He does, however, have car keys.

Honey, Mrs. Norwood says weakly. *Your arm.*

Your arm's nothing. It's fine. You can do the stitches later yourself. Mrs. Norwood doesn't seem assured by that and tries getting up again, but she's woozy from blood loss and almost passes out. Joey, squeezing her hand, bursts into tears. Neither tries to pull out the scissors. You love them impossibly.

But they can't want you, feral thing that you are, and even if they did…

No. You couldn't risk it. You won't.

The babysitter makes a small noise. Right, you forgot she was still alive. You should take money from her, too, since she hasn't done anything productive all night, but she wasn't actually shitty to you, and you feel bad, robbing some traumatized kid. You tell her it'll be okay. The ambulance is almost here. They'll all be okay, probably.

You don't have to leave, Joey says—
But you do. Of course, you do.

Here's the thing about leaving: you end up in a town ten minutes outside home because that's where Tyler's truck runs out of gas.

You hop out with some vague idea of making it to the gas station; instead, you end up at the cemetery where your mother is buried at. And your best friend. And your four other friends, and their boyfriends, too. You're still wearing the bloody pink pajamas from two days ago, but it's midnight and no one's around to notice. Anyway, the important thing is talking to your mom, but what can you say? *Sorry you're dead, Mom? Sorry I'm everything you didn't want me to be?*

You've never been able to risk getting drunk before. But right now? You need to get so drunk you don't even remember your own name.

So, you take your ten bucks and buy the cheapest bottle of whiskey you can find. The cashier is freaked out by your clothes, but he's also really high; plus, selling to a minor, so hopefully, he won't call the cops on you. You hike back to the truck and start drinking. It tastes like ass. You keep drinking. It doesn't taste so bad. You keep drinking. It doesn't taste like anything. You keep drinking.

Someone gets into the passenger seat. You're probably about to die.

The person becomes Mrs. Norwood. You think, anyway;

her face keeps rippling. A hallucination, then. That's nice. You can tell the truth to hallucinations; they already know all your secrets, anyway. You try and tell her lots of things, like what fire axes can do to human skulls or how you see your mom in your dreams sometimes, but her head splits open wider and wider each time she says she loves you. And then Mrs. Norwood's drinking from the bottle, which, when did she get the bottle? And you're outside somewhere, throwing up, and Mrs. Norwood's telling you it'll be okay, and you're lying down in the backseat of some car, and you can't see her, but she's still saying it.

You're okay, now. You're safe. Go to sleep. Go to sleep.

So you sleep.

Here's the thing about passing out in a car that you may or may not have hallucinated: you don't know where the fuck you are when you wake up, and Jesus Christ, you feel like shit. There's water next to your bed with a note that says DRINK ME, and you should absolutely not do that, but you're thirsty, so. If you open the door and get stabbed to death by a man in a Mad Hatter mask, you'll only have yourself to blame.

You open the door and are immediately attacked by six scrappy mutts. The smallest one only has three legs. You pick him up carefully and go downstairs.

Mrs. Norwood is in the kitchen, moving slowly. Carrying your drunk ass around couldn't have been any good for her shoulder. She serves you a plate of hangover food and only adds more each you time you protest. Eventually, you give up and eat it. *Where's Joey*, you ask.

At her Dad's, Mrs. Norwood tells you. We're probably going to move. You're going to come with us.

You almost choke on your food.

You tell her she doesn't need to do that. She gets you another bottle of water. You tell her she can help pay for your car. She says your car smells like piss and should be sold for parts immediately. You tell her you're fine. She says you're full of shit. You tell her you're dangerous. She says your Aunt Katherine's full of shit, too, and everyone else from your hometown, blaming a child for monsters in the night. You tell her you're eighteen, which is a year and three months from the truth. She says you're a child and retired from this life of chasing killers, at least until you graduate college. You tell her it was your choice to leave, your choice to fight, your choice to live the way you've been living. She looks at you real close and asks *was it*?

You start crying.

She lets you sob on her shoulder. *You're staying*, she tells you firmly, and eventually, you swallow and say, *okay*.

Here's the thing about sticking around: sometimes, it's hard not calling the shots. Sometimes, Mrs. Norwood's rules are stupid. Sometimes, you and Joey fight over the dumbest things. And killers do come back, occasionally: you go to some Christmas party and find a dead body underneath the tree, but Mrs. Norwood breaks through the door with a chainsaw, and Joey's aim with the rifle is really improving, and all you have to do is make cocoa and wipe blood off the presents. Sometimes, you're scared to touch your new family; sometimes, you think you should run away for their own good. But mostly, you institute Friday Movie Nights and eat whenever you want. Mostly, you get hugs before going to bed. Mostly, you keep adding to your five-year-plan.

THREE MAY KEEP A SECRET

THREE MAY KEEP A SECRET

S CARLETT ACCIDENTALLY WAKES the dead in the bottom of a coat closet, with a half-naked boy pressed against her and a bottle of tequila she's too drunk to drink[1]. That's all it is, in the end: flesh against flesh, and a few whispered secrets. A ghost story she swore she would never, ever tell.

It happens at one of Blake's parties. Blake is notorious for encouraging both bad decision-making and social equality: every student from every caste is welcome to drink and grope one another without fear of reprisal. Scarlett's social caste is invisible; it's beige paint and fall neutrals. Kids with names you remember whenever you need to borrow a pen. She should be home writing a paper about Benjamin Franklin; instead, she's here, graduating from Corona to Jose Cuervo,

1. Violence, child sexual abuse, child death, underage drinking.

and all because she'd heard Anna Pascal mention big Friday night plans. But Anna's not here. That was a totally facetious assumption to make. No, not facetious, she means... egregious? Specious? Something. She means... something.

She doesn't usually drink tequila. It's really not all that bad.

Only there's kind of a... blank spot where her memory should be, and now she's in the make-out closet with that new pretty boy from Spanish, only it's not the make-out closet when you're sixteen, is it? Scarlett's pretty sure it's the sex closet when you're sixteen, but that's a big deal for her, since she's never even kissed anyone, and now—now there is definite kissing; there are fingers fumbling with the button of her jeans, and Jesus, Jesus. The fingers she can't see are sliding under her panties, and they're—but she isn't —she isn't sure she wants this—

"Stop," Scarlett says into the boy's mouth. "Stop."

He pulls back. She can only see the barest outline of his face: angular, brown cheeks and askew hipster glasses. "O-okay. You okay?"

She doesn't know if she's okay.

"I'm okay," Scarlett says. "But I think, maybe, I don't—"

"Okay," the new kid says—Ibarra, Matt Ibarra. "That's okay." He stumbles backwards and thunks straight into a wall. His laughter is a little breathless. "But you think, not, we don't have to do anything, cause yeah, don't wanna be That Guy, just. My head's spinning, and...could we just sit here a minute, cause it's all...whatever out there. Bright, and...loud."

"We can sit," Scarlett says, because she doesn't want to deal with bright and loud things, either. Except... now she's just sitting here, with a boy, and someone's gonna have to say something. *Come on, Scar. Say something. Say something. Say—*

"You know any ghost stories?"

Because yes. That's where her stupid, morbid brain goes whenever she's somewhere dark, whenever she's somewhere small with no windows. This is why she will never have friends.

"Uh. No?"

"Cool," Scarlett says, because hey, who has time to be mortified when the whole room is spinning? "Yeah, I don't—"

"No, I do, I just can't. Uh. Put them in order, or remember. Anything. Um. You know some?"

Scarlett does. She collects them by the dozen, but the one on her tongue is the secret story. The last story.

You can't tell. Not ever, okay?

But Samantha's been dead a long time now, and it still hurts, keeping her words locked away.

"I can think of one," Scarlett says, and tells Matt all about the monster in the dark, the one who smells like cinnamon, the one with the flower petal hands.

She doesn't go home that night. She texts Mom she's staying at a friend's and then passes out across Matt's waist, waking with drool on her chin and a headache she can feel in her *bones*.

Scarlett sneaks out and, on the way home, prays to God that her text miraculously looks like something a halfway-sober person wrote.

God's not listening.

Later, after her mom decides to forego a grounding in favor of an uncomfortably frank sex talk that seems to go on for years, Scarlett spends the rest of the day recovering in her room, flipping through photo albums. She stops on an old Halloween picture: Scarlett had been dressed as Wonder Woman; Samantha, Indiana Jones. Sammy had wanted to be an archaeologist when she grew up. And a pilot. And a magician.

Scarlett doesn't think she's supposed to cry about things that happened nearly a decade ago, but she's tired and hungover and her best friend never became anything but bone dust. "Fuck it," she says, and rubs mercilessly at her eyes, eventually falling asleep with the picture still between her fingers.

In her dreams, they're eight years old again, and acrobats are flying through the air, soaring over dead elephants and broken peanut shells. "Come on!" Scarlett says, pointing at the Big Top. "I wanna learn how to become a superhero!"

But Sammy would rather be a magician. She grabs Scarlett by the hand, dragging her to an already full bathtub. "I can hold my breath forever," Sammy says. "It's an easy trick, see." And she pushes Scarlett into the tub and holds her down, down, down.

Scarlett wakes suddenly, out of breath and eyes wet… but someone else is crying too, a child's wail, high-pitched and gasping. "Scar," it says between hiccups. "Scar —*Scarlett*—"

Scarlett lunges for the light. The room is empty and silent.

Monday comes, unfortunately. Scarlett hopes Spanish won't be too awkward—seating is arranged alphabetically by fake Spanish name, so "Alejandro" shouldn't feel obligated to say anything to "Soledad" —but there's still the Moment of Truth when Matt walks in. Fortunately, he only stares for a half-second too long before walking to his seat. So. Okay. Scarlett exhales, a sigh that is more relief than regret, probably. She tries not to think about either him or Anna, who sits in front of Scarlett, her teal tank top clinging close to her ebony skin, scooping low in the back, inviting careful exploration.

Sitting on her hands would be noticeably weird, so Scarlett grips her pen as she copies conjugations. When the bell rings, she all but runs out of class.

That's when Matt promptly breaks their Unspoken Mutual Amnesia Pact.

"So," he says, sitting on the grass beside her in all his skinny jeans and slouchy hat and coffee shop hipster glory. "Here's the thing: being new and all, I kind of miss having friends to hang with? But I don't really know anyone except you, and—hey, if you can't be friends with the girl you drunkenly spooned with, I mean …"

Scarlett stares at him.

He winces. "I brought snacks?"

Well. She does like snacks. "Bribery seems like a good foundation for friendship," she says finally.

Matt brightens and opens his backpack. "Right?" He pulls out a bag of pretzels and drops it next to his coffee cup. "So, I was thinking I provide food. You let me hang sometimes and pretend I'm not a total loser. Doable?"

He offers both the pretzels and the coffee.

Scarlett takes the cup: she loves Wyatt's Coffee, goes there almost every day. "I'm not necessarily against this plan," she says. "But I should warn you, in case you're secretly blind: this isn't exactly the cool kids table."

Matt shrugs. "Whatever. Popular kids are boring. At least, that's what Mama's been telling me since it became stupidly obvious I wasn't cut out to be one." He cocks his head, peering down at her history outline. "I see you're going with the 'opening quote' approach. Bold move."

"Dick," Scarlett says, amiably enough. "It's a tried and true method. Besides, I've got a good one."

"Death and taxes?"

Scarlett shakes her head, tries out her best spooky voice. "Three may keep a secret," she says, "if two of them are dead."

That night, Scarlett dreams she's playing hide n' seek with Samantha, but when Sammy finds her in an empty tub, the tub is suddenly full and Scarlett's choking on bubbles and bathwater.

The next night she dreams she's back in Sammy's bathroom, lying on cold porcelain directly under the running faucet. Scarlett tries to get up, but she's paralyzed as tiny, dead fingers pry her lips apart, holding her mouth open wide.

She dreams of bathtubs everywhere: at school, on the lawn, even one in the middle of the highway. She stops her truck to investigate, only to find Sammy's pale, wet body inside—but when Scarlett tries to pull her out, Sammy pulls her in. Scarlett wakes from that one coughing into her pillow, and freezes when she hears something else wake with her.

You promised, a voice says. You promised you promised YOU BROKE YOUR PROMISE.

But it's not Sammy. It's not, because it can't be, because Sammy is dead and Scarlett doesn't believe in ghosts. It's all psychological, some weird, repressed guilt thing, and it'll pass because it has to.

It doesn't pass.

On Saturday, Scarlett wakes, fumbling for the light—but this time, the whispers don't fade, not until dawn. She doesn't even try sleeping on Sunday, just works on her laptop, headphones blasting—but the music keeps cutting out, replaced with the sound of water rushing from the tap.

She's in such bad need of caffeine come Monday morning that she drops by Wyatt's Coffee and orders herself two cups. Wyatt, himself, is manning the register, and he softly touches her wrist when he gives back her change.

She shakes her head at his concern. "It's nothing," she lies. "Big test." It's the kind of lie adults believe, and anyway, she can't exactly tell him that his dead niece has been drowning Scarlett in her sleep. Though she'd like to; anyone who still remembers Sammy talks like she's just a story. *Once there was a girl, and she died. It was very sad.* But Wyatt talks about Sammy the way Scarlett remembers her: bright, wild, alive. Scarlett can almost find the words, when Wyatt talks.

Outside, Scarlett runs into Matt. He raises his eyebrows, but politely doesn't ask about her new double-fisting habit. In return, she doesn't ask about the shadows under his eyes or the unhealthy sheen that's come over his golden brown skin. If bribery is a good foundation for friendship, then surely secrets are the key to keeping it alive.

You and Sammy didn't need secrets, Scarlett thinks to herself, and then shrugs it away. Of course they didn't. What kind of secrets did eight-year-olds even have?

"It's time," her mother says, and Scarlett follows her to the funeral. But when they get to the cemetery, they aren't lowering a coffin into the ground at all; it's a bathtub, and suddenly Scarlett's the one inside it. Sammy and the rest of the mourners stand by, black water buckets beside their feet.

"Don't do this! Sammy, please! Don't leave me down here!"

Sammy smiles. "And if I go and prepare a place for you," she says, "I will come back and take you with me."

"Sammy—"

"I'll take you with me," Sammy says, "that you may also be where I am."

The mourners upturn their buckets, and water fills the grave—

—and Scarlett wakes up, coughing so hard that she throws up over the side of the bed. She freezes, listening out, before remembering that her mom is still down at the firehouse. Shaking, Scarlett cleans up the mess, and jumps a foot in the air when her phone goes off. It's a text message from Matt. At 3:17 in the morning.

[Gotta GTFO of my house for a while. If ur still rocking hardcore insomnia wanna come? y/n]

Before she can even respond, another message comes through. [Holy shit that's creepy AF huh? Nm, nm. See you tomorrow. Promise not a serial killer]

Scarlett snorts softly. [Could use some fresh air,] she texts, since she sure as hell isn't going back to sleep now, or ever again. [Fair warning. May be going crazy.]

[It's going around. Meet up where?]

There's a diner about 15 minutes away that's open 24/7. She's about to send the address when she realizes she's already sent a different one. *Jesus*, she thinks. *No, no, not THERE.*

But Matt's already agreed, and Scarlett doesn't want to seem even crazier by vetoing her own suggestion, so she throws on her sweater and ratty sneakers. Her phone dings again, and she picks it up. This time, it's an unlisted number.

[YOU TOLD YOU TOLD YOU PROMISED NOT TO TELL]

Scarlett gasps and drops the phone. It cracks when it bounces against the floor. Water leaks from the screen.

Scarlett runs, leaving the phone behind.

The house is little and gray and hiding underneath a monstrous weeping willow. Scarlett sits on the dirty porch, staring at the picture of her and Sammy. It was in her sweater pocket. She doesn't remember putting it there.

"Hey."

Scarlett looks up. It's Matt, and he looks *terrible*, pale and hunched in on himself and moving slow, like things are broken inside. "Jesus," she says, half-standing. "Are you—"

"I'm fine," he says, waving her off, as he cautiously settles beside her and looks around. "So, I said let's hang, and you picked a porch on a totally abandoned house in the middle of nowhere. That...seems normal."

"Promise I'm not a serial killer either?"

"Don't buy it," Matt says. "But nobody's perfect, I guess."

Scarlett tries to smile.

She must not do a very good job because he frowns. "Hey. Are you okay?"

She laughs.

"So, that's a no, then."

Scarlett rests her head on her knees. "Last week my biggest problem was having a crush on the most popular girl in school, and whether to come out to my mom as maybe-sorta-quasi bi."

Matt raises his eyebrows. "Maybe-sorta-quasi?"

"Well. Cause mostly I like guys—" Scarlett remembers Matt's fingers under her panties and realizes that she's actually not too exhausted to blush. "But, uh. There's this one girl, Anna. It's really just her, so I don't know if it counts, and I don't really wanna say anything yet, even though my mom's pretty awesome, and she'd be all awkwardly supportive, but…it just feels like a lot. You know?"

"Yeah," Matt says. "I mean, technically, no. I'm pretty straight. Like Idris Elba could come up, and I'd be like nah, man. But sure, my mom's the best, and I'd still be freaked about saying, 'Hey, BT dubs, I'm kinda gay. Thoughts?'"

She looks at him. "You think?"

"Yeah." Matt says. "I mean, I get you on perspective— last week, I was just worried about failing that Spanish quiz…that's today, right?"

"Yeah."

"Shit, I'm fucked. But that's what I'm saying: last week total panic; this week, well. I've got other stuff this week. But even if you *were* 100% on the bisexuality train instead of the bicurious go-cart, and your mom was handing out 'I'm Down With the Gay' buttons left and right, like, you don't gotta rush anything you're not ready for. Don't have to justify that shit with reasons, either. Some secrets are okay to keep."

Maybe. But Scarlett thinks she's holding onto one too many secrets. How do you know when to release them? How do you know when it's *safe*?

She glances back at the photo in her hand, and Matt grins. "Look at Tiny Scarlett, busting a move with the Lasso of Truth. Girl Indy...is that Anna?"

That's almost funny. "Sammy," Scarlett corrects. "She was my friend, my best friend. She used to live here."

Matt's grin fades as he looks around at the cracked porch and dust-covered windows. "How did she die?"

Scarlett stares straight ahead, and she's so exhausted that her vision is blurring. If she squints, she can see a bathtub on the lawn.

"She drowned," Scarlett whispers, and closes her eyes.

"You don't have to—"

"She slipped, hit her head. Her parents found her too late. They never got over it, packed up and moved out of town. Wyatt stayed—Sammy's uncle—but he doesn't live *here*. People never live here long. Six months, maybe, and they're out."

"It's haunted?"

Matt's voice is hushed. Scarlett's startled to realize he's trembling, with a wary eye out on the front door.

"I don't think so," Scarlett says; after all, Samantha isn't haunting the *house*. "There aren't any sightings, anyway. People just...never seem to stay. Matt, I'm sorry."

He blinks at her. "For what?"

Freaking you out. "Just...for dumping this all on you. Maybe I should stop telling you ghost stories."

30

Matt smiles, and it's hard to read. "I do spook easy," he says bitterly, and staggers when he tries to stand. Scarlett jumps up to catch him, and he leans against a post for support.

"Jesus, Matt, are you—"

"I'm fine."

She stares at him. He's slightly out of breath and grimacing, and she suddenly wishes she knew more, or anything, about him. His mom might be the best, but he didn't say anything about his dad, and maybe that's just because his split like hers, or maybe ...

"Matt," Scarlett says. "Look, if someone's, you know, hurting you—"

He snorts. "Save your pamphlets. I'm fine. All I really need is some sleep, and for someone to teach me Spanish so I can stop disappointing my grandparents every time we visit."

"Well, I definitely can't help with that," Scarlett says, watching him not quite meet her gaze. "But after we both fail the quiz today—maybe we can study together? Talk about girls?"

He looks at her finally, even smiles a little. "It's a date," Matt says.

But he never shows up to school.

Scarlett texts Matt fourteen times and actually calls him twice. Maybe he just overslept, but...she can't shake the worry. She should never have let him drive off; he was out of breath from trying to *stand up*. Something's wrong. Maybe he's choking to death, maybe he's already dead—

[14 messages? Damn girl. Thought I was popular for half a sec]

Scarlett immediately calls him again.

"Look," Matt says, answering. "I'm—"

"Don't tell me you're okay," Scarlett says, crossing the parking lot and throwing her books in the back of her truck. "I won't believe it. What's wrong?"

"I'm just, I'm." Matt's sigh becomes a wheeze, which becomes stifled coughing. "Sore, that's all. It's not a big—"

"Matt?" Scarlett hops into the driver's seat. "Some secrets aren't so great to keep."

There's a long pause. "I can't tell you," Matt says finally, and his voice sounds raw, scratched and bloody. "Not this, Scarlett. I want to, but you wouldn't believe me. *I* wouldn't believe me."

She considers bursting into hysterical laughter. "Trust me," she says. "At this point, I'd..."

Holy SHIT.

It can't be. It can't be, but...the timing of it all. And he looked so scared, back at the house. He looked—

"Scarlett?"

"Matt," she says quickly, to keep from second-guessing herself. "Are you being haunted?"

Another long pause—and then, Christ, Matt *whimpers*. "You—how can you know that?"

"Long story. But I guess that's what got us into this."

"What—"

"Give me your address," Scarlett says. "We need to talk."

Matt lives in a pretty nice part of town, the kind of place where all the houses look the same and there are restrictions on what color and size your lawn gnomes can be. He answers the door in a worn, gray hoodie and bare feet, looking about five seconds from tears. She hugs him without thinking, and he holds on even as he grunts a little. "Are your parents home?" she whispers.

He lets go. "It's just Mom and me," he says. "And no. Took forever, convincing her to leave. She thinks my ribs are bust."

"Are they?"

"Maybe. But you don't seem so bad off. Hasn't it—"

Scarlett frowns. "*It*?"

Matt takes a faltering step back. "Yeah, you said, I thought you …" He's breathing too fast, and each breath is a whistle, air drawn through a straw. "Scar, please don't be screwing with me. Please, I can't—"

"Hey, hey. It's okay." She takes him by the hand and is startled by how cold his fingers are. "I'm not screwing with you, I swear." She guides him into the living room, sinking down on the couch.

"Samantha told me," Scarlett says. "That story, she told it to me the day she died, said it was a secret, but I never thought anything like this…she's haunting me, Matt, but you—what the hell is haunting you?"

Matt does start crying then.

"It's the ghost from the story, Scar. It's the monster with the flower petal hands."

"You can't tell," Samantha said. "Not ever, okay?"

They were in Sammy's bathroom, sitting on the floor with the door closed and the lights off, squeezing each other's hands to keep from getting lost. It was silly, but sometimes Scarlett thought-pretended that the room grew in the dark, that if she lost her friend's hand, she'd never find it again. Sometimes, Scarlett thought-pretended that all the ghost stories were real.

"Not ever," she said.

"Okay." Sammy's voice shook. "Once upon a time, there was a lonely monster who lived in a cellar, a, a candy shop cellar. The monster wanted a friend, but it was all dark fur and teeth, and it knew the kids in the candy shop would be scared of it. But the monster was still lonely, so one night it followed a little girl home, and when she went to bed, it wanted to play. She could only smell it at first, cause it smelled like sweet things, like cinnamon, and its fur was too dark to see. But then the monster touched the girl, and she could see its hands. They were soft, like, like flower petals.

"The monster was happy to finally play with a friend, but it didn't know how to play right. The petals touched the girl all over, sucking up her soul. The girl was real pretty, and her soul was bright and special. The monster kept coming back, and the girl hid, but eventually it found her. It fed and fed until she died, and the monster realized it had never been lonely at all, just hungry. So, the monster went

looking for other kids, pretty kids with bright, shiny souls, and if you don't wanna be one—you don't wanna be one, right?"

"Right," Scarlett whispered.

"Then be ugly," Samantha said, squeezing Scarlett's fingers tighter. "Be ugly and ordinary and not special at all, or the monster with the flower petal hands is gonna eat you, too."

"I don't get it," Scarlett says, leaning forward on the couch. "Sammy haunts me for breaking the promise, fine. But you, it's, it's just a *story*."

Matt shakes his head. "Maybe it was once, I don't know. But it's more than that now. Like, like one of those horror movies. Watch the wrong video, play the wrong game, read the wrong text, boom, you're dead."

"But I heard the story eight years ago," Scarlett says, "and nothing came after me. And Sammy...nothing ate her. She *drowned*." That, at least, Scarlett knows for sure: even now, the back of her neck feels damp, like water is trickling down from her hair. She tries to wipe it away. "Are you *sure*—"

Matt nods. "It comes at night. I can't see its fur or teeth, but its hands, its hands ..."

He's shaking again. She hands him a box of Kleenex.

Matt wipes his eyes. "Its hands really are flower petals, these big, red weeping ones. Creepy soft. When it touched my face..." Matt shudders. "If I don't fight back, it almost doesn't hurt. I'm just sick and exhausted. But if I do?" He lifts his shirt up, and she stares at the horrific spread of black and purple stretching across his torso.

"Jesus, Matt."

Matt almost smiles. "Yeah. And it's weird, but it really does smell like cinnamon. My mom made hot chocolate this morning, and I almost fucking lost it."

"What did you tell her?"

"About the new body art? Bullies." He chucks the Kleenex at the coffee table—it bounces straight off—and sinks back into the couch. "I tried hiding. It worked once, but the next night the monster found me. It's just gonna keep finding me, and I don't, I don't know how much soul I've got left to give."

She squeezes his too-cold hand tighter. He squeezes back, but his grip is weak.

"Okay," she says. "You need to sleep at my place tonight."

Matt stares at her.

"Hide there. Maybe the monster won't look for you in my room. Give us more time to think of…something."

"Um," Matt says. "Won't your mom have a problem with that? Cause, you know, school night. And genitals."

Scarlett does not giggle at that, and if she does, it's only because of insomnia-induced hysteria. "Possibly," she says, "but I'll figure it out. I promise, Matt. I'm gonna fix this."

"Hey." Matt leans into her. "This isn't your fault."

Scarlett closes her eyes. "It is." Somehow, she knows it is.

She goes home and makes dinner. Mom, only just waking up after her 24-hour shift, is justifiably suspicious.

"Let me throw some water on my face, kid," she says. Scarlett's ladling macaroni into plastic bowls by the time Mom comes back, arms crossed. "You're not pregnant, right?"

"*Mom.*"

"Hey, I'm just checking."

Scarlett shakes her head, sits down at the table, and makes her pitch. Mom is halfway through her macaroni before she finally says, "This your boyfriend?"

"No."

"You want him to be?"

Scarlett pauses, takes an especially long sip of milk. "No," she says finally. Matt's a good guy, and she likes guys; she's certain about that much at least, but she doesn't think she wants to date him, either. "But he's going through a rough time right now, and I wanna, you know. Help."

"And how are *you* doing right now?"

Scarlett blinks, and Mom snorts. "Scar. I try my best to give you space, but I'm not an idiot. You've haven't slept with the lights on since you were six, and with the drinking—"

"Okay, that was a one- time thing," Scarlett says, which is the truth, mostly.

"And the sleeping?"

"...bad dreams, I guess." She pushes her macaroni around. "I've been thinking about Sammy a lot, lately."

Mom stops, and sets down her fork, which is not a thing

that happens when Velveeta is on the table. "You don't talk much about Sammy."

"I know," Scarlett says. "I…"

But the words get stuck in her throat. All these years with Sammy gone, and Scarlett's never known how to explain that Sammy isn't just an old picture, a ghost story, a tragic event that Scarlett overcame. Wyatt knows, but Wyatt only likes to talk about the good times, and some days she just *can't*. Samantha was her best friend, and was stolen away. She's an open wound that never fully stopped bleeding.

And now…

"Hey." Mom reaches over and squeezes Scarlett's hand, which—for Mom—is the equivalent of a giant bear hug. "You know you can talk to me, kid."

I want to, Scarlett thinks bitterly. It hurts, how much she wants to. *But you wouldn't believe me. I wouldn't believe me.*

"I know." She clears her throat. "So, can Matt stay over?"

Mom sighs, and releases Scarlett's hand. "Bedroom door open," is all she says.

Matt comes over an hour later. Mom eyes him for a while before eventually shoving store-bought cake at his face and shooing them off. Matt blinks at the cake as Scarlett drags him to her bedroom. "It's a good sign," she says.

"Yeah?"

"You look pretty pathetic. Need feeding. Way too weak to jump my bones."

"Great," Matt says sourly as he collapses on her bed. "That's, oh. Maybe I should, uh, the floor—"

"Relax," Scarlett says, amused. "I'm not sleeping anyway."

But she does, of course. She's just so goddamned tired: one second she's at her desk, and the next she's in the bathtub, Sammy on the ceiling above her. A flood of water pours down from her long blonde hair.

"Bad things! BAD THINGS! *BAD THINGS!*"

"Scarlett!"

Scarlett wakes, choking—and immediately coughs up a mouthful of water. *No, that's not, it's not possible—*

Matt's kneeling at her side. Hesitatingly, he reaches out. His fingers graze her lips and come away wet. "Holy shit," he breathes—

And then the lights go out.

Scarlett stands, and something grabs her hand. No, not something, Matt. He pulls, and she's not expecting it, tumbles forward to her hands and knees. "Matt," she says, but he doesn't hear her, can't, maybe, over the sound of his own breathing: in, out, in, out, in, in, in, in. He pulls again, frantically, and she knocks her head against the bed frame before she figures out what he's doing.

Scarlet crawls under the bed, pressed up against him. She can just make out his hipster glasses, his angular cheeks, and his hands, clamped tight over his mouth. She starts to say his name—

But then she smells it. Cinnamon.

Scarlett can't hear the monster, but she knows it's there, looking. A red petal drifts to the floor, then another. Any second it might kneel down, duck under and reach…

But eventually the cinnamon fades, and it's just her and Matt again.

"Matt. Matt?"

Matt just clings to her, crying. She clings right back, and they stay like that until dawn, until sunlight drives both their ghosts away.

"Fuck school," Matt says the next day. "We're going to the library."

She drives slowly, in case she has to dodge any phantom bathtubs. Then Matt falls getting out of the truck. They're quite a pair.

"Let's pretend it *is* a cursed story," he says, as she helps him inside. "There's gotta be records or something, right? Weird local shit?"

He Googles "weird local shit," while Scarlett looks up ghosts in the non-fiction section. She feels ridiculous and gives up an hour later, sitting next to Matt. His color is better today, but his skin is cold. The desk might be the only thing keeping him upright.

"Anything?"

Matt shakes his head. "No mysterious deaths. No ghost sightings. Shit, there's not even a candy store for 70 miles." He crosses his arms. "This town is bullshit."

"Well, maybe it's an old story," Scarlett says. "Like, I don't know. From Europe, or something."

"Maybe? But I still can't find it. Monsters in the dark, but not cinnamon. Clawed hands, but not petal ones. It's like…someone just made it up."

"I didn't—"

"I know. But maybe Sammy did."

"No," Scarlett says. "No. She was scared, Matt. Why would she be scared of a story she made up?"

Matt shrugs. "I don't know. But if she knew what could happen, why did she even tell you?"

Scarlett doesn't know. She doesn't understand the ghost story at all. It's never fit in her collection, doesn't function the way a ghost story should. The monster was never dead. The monster was never wronged. It's not seeking revenge or punishing the wicked. It's looking for other kids instead: pretty kids, special kids. You have to be ordinary and ugly to escape it. What the hell kind of moral is that?

Maybe it's not a ghost story, Scarlett thinks. Maybe it's something else.

If a monster like that was real, it would've hunted Samantha down for sure. She was smart, fearless. Samantha was one of the bright and loud things.

And Matt …

"You're pretty," Scarlett says.

"Uh. Thanks?"

He is, though. He's pretty, and he's loud: he talks all the damn time. He's too weird to be popular. He's a coffee shop hipster, and he shines.

Is that how the monster found him? Is that why it crept into his room and…and touched him all…

Oh God.

Bad things happen if you tell.

Samantha told. Samantha told a story, but it was never a ghost story at all, was it? And Scarlett, she hadn't understood, but now—

"Scarlett? You okay?"

No. She's really not.

But she does make it to the bathroom before she throws up.

"Scarlett," Matt says anxiously when she returns. "What—"

Scarlett swallows. "I think I need to tell another ghost story, after all."

They wait until midnight, and then break into the house. Scarlett leads Matt into the bathroom. It's even smaller than she remembers. Thin slivers of moonlight stretch from the living room window. When she closes the door, even that is gone.

Blindly, she reaches forward and finds Matt's hand. She squeezes his cold fingers, suddenly afraid of getting lost in the dark.

"Once upon a time," Scarlett says, voice shaking, "a little girl lived in this house, and something was hurting her. Someone."

Water trickles down her spine again. Scarlett shudders, and Matt squeezes her hand.

"What happened next?" he asks, even though it's an old story, a depressingly old, familiar story.

"The person hurting her was a monster, but not the kind of monster with fur and teeth. His hands were flesh, not petals, and they…they touched where they shouldn't touch."

Weeping. Scarlett tries to ignore it. "He probably told her things to keep her quiet. Said he was lonely, needed a friend. Said she was too pretty, too special. He tried to make it her fault, but Sammy, it never was."

Matt inhales sharply. "Scarlett."

She can smell it too. Two ghosts with them now: one real, one made real.

"Stop," Samantha whispers from behind her. "Bad things happen if you tell."

But she has to tell, otherwise it will never end, not for any of them. "The little girl was scared. She didn't know how to make it stop. I don't think she couldn't accept that it was a *person* hurting her. So she made up a story that made more sense. She told it to her best friend."

Something groans behind her, something rusted that doesn't want to give—and then a rush of water. "That, it *can't*," Matt says desperately. "The water can't be turned on, it's not—"

But the water *is* on, and it's loud. Scarlett yells to hear herself over it.

"Her best friend didn't understand. She didn't—she didn't tell anyone, and the little girl went home and…

maybe, maybe he *did* come by, but I think, I think it was just an accident. I think she just—"

Samantha screams, so loud the room shakes and something explodes above them, breaking glass, cascading shards—the mirror, Scarlett realizes, and tries to cover her head. Matt pulls back, swearing, and before she can reach out again, something's wrapped around her arms: cold, tiny fingers digging into her skin and dragging her backwards. Towards the tub.

Scarlett's the one screaming now.

She tries to grab onto something, but there's nothing to hold onto. Samantha drags her effortlessly, lifts her up and rolls her over—and then Scarlett's splashing face first into the water She bucks back, kicking frantically, trying to push herself up—and finally breaks through, coughing so hard she can barely hear Matt across the room. "Matt," Scarlett tries to say, and is pushed under the water again.

Her lungs are squeezing shut. She can't breathe. She can't *breathe.*

She manages to lift up on her elbows again. "Sammy, Sammy stop. Please, you have to stop."

"You promised," Samantha says. "You promised you wouldn't tell!"

"I *should* have told," Scarlett says, trying to get to her knees. She slips, nearly goes under. "Sammy, I—"

But there's a strange thumping sound she can't identify, something smacking against wood. "Mother. Fucking. *Christ,*" Matt says, and suddenly Scarlett can see, as the bathroom door swings open and moonlight filters through the room.

It's hard to see it, the thing crouching over Matt. A glimpse of teeth that vanish, black fur that disappears into the shadows...but she can see hands floating in the darkness. Its long fingers are pale and smooth.

Its long fingers transform into rose petals as they crawl over the back of Matt's neck.

Matt gasps and tries to pull himself forward, but the petals fall from nowhere: sliding under his shirt, weighing him down, leeching him. He breathes in short, reflexive gulps. The pauses between them grow longer and longer.

Scarlett pushes up from the tub, hard as she can, and rolls onto her back.

Samantha, above her, doesn't flicker from sight. She just stands there, a dead little girl with wet, tangled, blonde hair and blood-burst eyes. "Bad things," she whispers. "Bad things, bad things."

"Not because you told," Scarlett says. "You need to hear the rest of the story."

"No," Samantha says, and attacks—but Scarlett's prepared this time, catches her by the wrists.

"The little girl died," Scarlett said, "but she didn't rest, not really. I think maybe she hid right here in this house, hid from the monster she believed in so much, the monster that she took with her. I hope—" Her voice broke. "Christ, I hope it never found her, that it wasn't, wasn't hurting her all that time. I hope she just curled up and slept under the bed for eight years. Until, until her best friend broke a promise and woke the girl, and the monster too."

"No," Samantha says, letting go and putting her hands over her ears. "No, I don't want to hear."

But it's almost done now, and it has to be Samantha who finishes it.

Scarlett can't hear Matt anymore.

She doesn't look. She can't look.

"The monster went after a new kid, just like in the story. But the little girl, she forgot that she'd made up the story. She kept the secret so long she forgot the monster, *this* monster, wasn't real. You have to name the real monster, Sammy. You have to say it out loud."

"I can't," Samantha says, sobbing. "He'll hurt me if I tell."

Scarlett grabs her hands, squeezes tight. "It's the secret, that's hurting you," she says. "And you don't have to keep it for him anymore. You don't have to be scared anymore."

"Scarlett—"

"Please tell me, Sammy. Tell me who the real monster is."

Sammy clings to her. She screams into Scarlett's shirt: "Uncle Wyatt, Uncle Wyatt, *Uncle Wyatt!*"

And everything suddenly stops.

There's no sound, no sound at all, but Scarlett's heartbeat and Sammy's tears. Scarlett hugs her desperately.

"I'm so, so sorry, Sammy. I didn't tell, I didn't know—"

"I was so scared—"

"I should've known—"

"I didn't want it—"

"I should've *known*."

Scarlett closes her eyes, weeping. She should have, she could have—

"I'm going to tell," Sammy whispers. "I think I'm ready to tell now."

Scarlett opens her eyes then—but Samantha's just gone.

The water is gone, too, although Scarlett's still wet. The scent of cinnamon has vanished, flower petals too, and Matt—

"No," Scarlett says, gracelessly scrambling out of the tub. "Matt!"

She crawls forward, grabbing him by the arm and pushing him on his back. Shaking him. "Matt, please don't be dead. Wake up, don't be dead, don't be dead, don't be—"

"Not," Matt says faintly. His eyes flicker open. "Don't think, anyway." He tries to lift his head off the floor, fails. "Is it over?"

"I—I don't know. She just, she—I think so. I think so?" Scarlett shakes her head. "Can you move?"

"Yeah, totally," Matt says. "Any second now." He pauses. "Or. Alternatively. We could just, can we just—"

"Sit here a minute?" Scarlett asks, and collapses beside him. "Yeah. It's all whatever out there anyway. We can sit. We can definitely sit."

On Monday she goes back to school.

It seems horrifically unfair that she still has to deal with pop quizzes and P.E. after nearly dying, but no one accepts 'a ghost ate my homework', and she can't fake a cold forever. Matt seems to be doing okay with it, anyway, after sleeping for two days straight. He even gets an A on his makeup quiz. Scarlett's paper on Benjamin Franklin, meanwhile, is turned in two days late for a C-. Fuck it.

She still isn't sleeping well. She keeps waking up in the middle of the night, tense and shaking, but lonely too, when nothing else wakes with her. Scarlett misses Samantha. She wants to know her best friend's okay now.

A couple of days later, Scarlett decides she is.

There are whispers around town that Wyatt's Coffee is haunted, stories about a dead girl who disappears when you blink, who sits at your table and drips water on the floor. When the Muzak cuts out, the speakers hiss a name: *Uncle Wyatt. Uncle Wyatt. Uncle Wyatt.*

It's all just ghost stories. Rumors, pranks—nobody really believes the whispers, not even the whisperers themselves. Ghosts aren't real, after all, and there's a rational explanation for everything. Which doesn't explain why the shop's deserted when Scarlett walks in.

Wyatt is at the counter, eyes bloodshot and wet. Scarlett orders a mocha, which he spills twice in the process of making.

She doesn't pay for it, doesn't take the cup, never wants their skin to touch again.

"I know what you did," Scarlett says. "And everyone here, whether they can admit it or not, whether they can prove it or not...they know too. Everyone knows what you are."

Wyatt shudders. He looks to the left, shudders again, and opens his mouth.

But Scarlett doesn't need to hear anything he has to say.

She turns and sees Samantha sitting at the far table, staring at Wyatt. Scarlett holds out her hand, inclines her head. *Come with me, Sammy. Come home.*

But Sammy just smiles and shakes her head.

"I'm not done talking yet," she says, and Scarlett has to accept that.

"When you are," Scarlett says. "I'll be around."

She leaves the coffee shop, and behind her, Wyatt weeps.

Meanwhile, life continues, and with that—

"Homecoming," Matt says, as he stands up from her kitchen table and packs his books away. "Are you going to ask Anna?"

Anna probably doesn't even know Scarlett's name. She does know her fake Spanish name, because she used it the other day. Asking for a pen. "I don't think we're quite at dance level," Scarlett says. "I thought maybe I'd just try, you know, saying hi instead. Doesn't sound as scary as it used to."

"Well, it probably can't get drowning-in-your-sleep bad."

"That's what I'm saying." Scarlett hears her mom pull up and instinctively takes a breath. "I'm still not exactly sure where I fit, like, I don't think I wanna tell Mom I'm ..."

"Maybe-sorta-quasi bi?" Matt asks, smiling. "Sure. Just, you know it doesn't have to be a 50/50 split, right? Like, pretty sure the bisexuality train is not a rollercoaster: you don't gotta be this much gay to ride."

Scarlett laughs. "I'll keep it in mind," she says.

Mom comes in with a half dozen grocery bags on each arm. Matt helps out before taking off, leaving Scarlett standing alone, standing around helplessly. She's rehearsed sixteen different conversation starters; none of them were "so, want me to make dinner?" But apparently, that's what she's going with.

Mom looks at her, sighs. "Let me take my boots off, kid."

Scarlett scoops chili into a pan while she waits. She'll tell Mom about the bi stuff, eventually, but...she needs a little time, and anyway, that secret isn't hurting her, not yet.

Mom walks back into the kitchen and squeezes Scarlett's hand: her bear hug, her wordless love. "Whatever you want to tell me," Mom says, "it's safe."

Scarlett takes a deep breath.

"It's about Sammy," she says. "I'm ready to tell now."

YOU WERE ONCE WILD HERE

YOU WERE ONCE WILD HERE

L AURA IS A *dead girl's name*[1]. That's your first thought when she introduces herself, all smiles, telling you about cheerleader tryouts like you aren't dressed from head to toe in get-the-fuck-away-from-me. Pretty blondes like her are always ending up dead somewhere, in lakes or forests, murdered by someone who insists they did it out of love. No point getting attached to a walking dead girl like that. No point getting attached, period: a few months and your parents will catch a new case, and you'll be on the road again. It's better this way: in any relationship, you prefer to do the leaving.

But of course, you do get attached. And of course, Laura ends up in that lake.

---

1. Violence, death, loss of a sibling, trauma, intimate partner abuse.

Your father finds the body. It's what he does best: dead flesh sings to him, beckons him forward to the dark and lonely places where corpses wait to be unearthed. It's four a.m. when he finds her, but you don't realize it, not then: you're at home, asleep, dreaming of Laura and the moon.

She's sitting beside you in a canoe, half naked. There's nothing sexual about it: your crushes are all fictional characters, heroines in lipstick and menswear, and anyway, you've never had a sex dream before. It would be strange to start with Laura, who's beautiful but miserable, who only laughs to change the subject and smiles at anyone she's scared of. She stopped smiling at you three weeks ago, when you told her that you're ace.

The moon is impossibly large. It takes up half the sky.

"I'm a werewolf," Laura says. "Did you know?"

You didn't, and it worries you: keeping tabs on people is your best subject at school, the only strategy that makes sense in the dog-eat-dog world of public education, where mean girls taunt queer kids into suicide and every gym teacher is a monster, often literally. Missing that your one and only friend is a lycanthrope? That's a red F, especially for you: the whole reason you're in this sad California backwater is so your mom can stop the werewolf killing off the student body.

But then, you and Laura have always been so careful to speak around your secrets. *We move around a lot*, but never why you move around. *My brother died*, but not what killed him, not what your mother sacrificed to avenge him. Not what lives inside her now. Something has always lived inside Laura, too, something reckless and dangerous, hidden under pastels and repression. Maybe you got too dependent. Maybe you just didn't want to know.

Laura's bleeding: a straight line from neck to pelvis. Even her hair is dripping blood, droplets that dye the lake dark red. She doesn't seem to notice. Her eyes are still on the moon.

"I had to do it. You'll understand by the end."

Spoken like the guilty. You really shouldn't warn her: the murders have been grisly but methodical, a monster who means to kill. If it's Laura, she deserves everything that's coming. But.

We could run away together. We could leave it all behind.

"Don't tell me any secrets," you say. "I know things I shouldn't in dreams."

But Laura doesn't listen. "The witch is on the squad. The proof is in the pocket. The confession is under the pew."

"Laura—"

Laura finally turns. Her skin isn't the same white as yours; it's ethereal, beaded with lake water. "You'll find me, won't you? Promise you'll find me, Emily."

But by the time you wake, it's dawn, and your dad already knows exactly where to find Laura.

You tell your parents about the dream, most of it. They hear the words "proof" and "pocket" and take off, leaving you with black coffee and powdered donuts for breakfast, and only asking if you knew Laura as an afterthought. They've always been happy that you're a loner. It's safer, they say, if you don't make friends. It's not that they're bad parents; they're just not great ones. They love you so much they can't help but fail.

You love them too, of course. It's why you've stopped begging to go along on stakeouts; it's why you've never snuck out to a party. It's why you'll never tell them anything you're actually thinking. And when Laura—intense and glittering and mysteriously, surreptitiously drunk at ten in the morning—grabbed your hand in the back of church and asked you to run away with her, it's why you said *let's wait till spring* instead of *yes, God yes, we could be free.*

She'd laughed, said *you'll miss the sermon,* as if coming to church had been your idea in the first place. Laura had very complicated rules about when and where you two could meet; she may have been your only friend, but you certainly weren't hers. You were Laura's goth little secret, kept hidden far from view. It didn't bother you: standing up for your true friends was a sucker's game when those friends would split town by Christmas. Laura was a survivor. You respected that.

But Laura didn't survive, and you can't just sit here, drinking coffee and waiting for your parents to return home with another dead monster to bury. Your dreams happen for a reason. They happen to *you* for a reason. Proof is something your mom needs—she won't make a kill without it, no matter how much the beast inside her threatens and claws for release—but it's not what you're looking for.

You're not sure what you're looking for, but "pocket" means zilch to you.

But then, that's not all Laura said.

The witch is on the squad. The confession is under the pew.

The pew is at St. Vivian, and the only squad that matters in this town? The Kiss-Kiss Girls.

Your parents don't understand these things. No point in telling them now. Laura is dead, but she still needs something from you.

First, you need something from her, too.

It's a mistake, of course.

She's not the first dead body you've seen. Your parents freak over your physical safety, but a little emotional damage is just common sense: how will you learn to steer clear of monsters if you don't see just how much flesh they can pull away with their teeth? And dead monsters have to be disposed of quickly. More hands on deck means less time red-handed. You've held what's left of the bodies, once your mother has completed her work.

But this is different; this is Laura. This is—

Part of the job. You wanted to be a detective, didn't you? Morgues are for clues, not closure, and Laura is a case file now.

It's the only way to survive.

So. Laura Young. 18. Kiss-Kiss Girl. Werewolf. Found in

the lake, a few feet from shore. Viciously torn apart: torso split open, neck to pelvis, and covered in claw marks. Bitemarks, too. The rib cage shattered; the sternum snapped straight in half. Face untouched, no defensive wounds. Bled out in ankle-high water. How long did it take? How long did she suffer?

There's something strange about the claw marks.

You can't quite figure what. You blink, but then it's not a body anymore, just piles of inside-out meat and chunks of things still tucked inside. Organs, they used to be organs, and you can see them, and you can *smell*—

You don't make it outside before you vomit up Hostess: bile and white powder, everywhere. Can't be helped now. Hastily, you clean it up and take off before Sheriff-Coroner Valento comes back, not that you expect him soon: the whole sheriff's department is a dangerous mix of incompetent, understaffed, racist, and corrupt, and the morgue—about the size of your parents' RV—is often left unattended. Breaking in was child's play. Literally: you could've done this when you were nine.

Your dad texts as you hop on your bike. Third text in an hour. It's always one of your parents, even when you're at school: [everything ok,] they ask; *are you alive,* they mean, and sometimes, there's this quaking inside you, this unsteady, vibrating force that threatens to explode—but you get it. Today, especially, you get it.

It was your father, of course, who found your brother's body, piece by bloody piece. Really, it's surprising your parents are as sane as they are.

[Emily, everything ok?]

[Safe at home,] you tell him, and ride your bike to St. Vivian.

The locks are better at St. Vivian. Have to like a town where the church has better security than the cooler. Six seconds more, and you'd have gotten it; instead, Father Gene nearly opens the door in your face, with the flushed and very married Mrs. Wickman two steps behind. Both are immediately defensive at the sight of you. *We were just* and *why aren't you* and *I won't report you to the principal this time.* Infidelity is so predictable, so sweaty, so boring.

You let Father Gene think he's blackmailing you, rather than the other way around, then get what you wanted in the first place: the church all to yourself. You sit in the back pew, just like the last time you saw Laura alive. The confession is scrawled on pink pages and taped underneath the seat.

No one will understand this. Maybe no one will even find it. Message in a bottle, lost at sea. Probably for the best.

Five people are dead. He said it's because he loves me, but that's not what love is. Please believe that I wanted to stop him. I thought if I was perfect, I could keep him from killing anyone else, but I don't know how to pretend anymore. I think I'm going crazy. It's like I can feel my blood all the time, like any second I might start screaming and never stop. He doesn't want me like that. He'll turn on me eventually.

I know I should have told someone. But no one will take my word over his, and anyway, nobody believes in werewolves. I have to leave. I have to do it tonight.

If you find this, take some free advice: don't trust anybody who uses their love to tame you. And if Emily Abbott is still around, tell her I'm sorry I couldn't wait. I think she'll understand. I think we both knew it always had to be this way.

With shaking fingers, you fold the letter in half, and half again, and slide it into your backpack.

We could run away together, she'd said, words breathy, desperate. You could smell the booze on her lips. We could leave it all behind. Go anywhere we want. Be anything we want.

But running takes money that neither of you have, and anyway, your dad would collapse. Your mom would lose control. A lot of people could die. It's a terrible power, being the only thing keeping your parents alive.

Would Laura still be alive if you'd said yes?

It's too much right now. You can't think about it.

Your phone chimes.

[Everything's fine, Mom. Find the killer?]

[Jake Valento. You know him?]

Well. That's predictable.

Jake Valento. 18. QB. Smug asshole. Abusive killer werewolf, apparently, and the Sheriff's only son. AKA, Emily's boyfriend.

You've watched him, of course. Taken a few pics. Entitled, aggressive, a charmer, like every other football god you've ever met. But your paths rarely crossed: you didn't share any classes, and Laura would never have allowed you two to talk.

Suffer with me at church, she'd said, when she'd meant *Jake won't see us here*. Laura hadn't been protecting herself. She'd been protecting you all along.

[Early suspect but had alibi. Proof now it's fake. Hunting him down. Not at the HS. Dad got arrested.]

[WHAT?]

[Arguing w/ cops. They caught real wolf in woods, insist it's the killer. You know your father.]

You do. It's one of the things you like best about him. He's not much of a fighter——the actual monster killing is all Mom—but look sidewise at an animal, and he'll do his best to fuck your shit up. [Need me to bail him out?]

[Not yet. Doing some UC from jail. Need to confirm Sheriff is just incompetent, not involved. May be out late. Money for pizza in drawer.]

You sigh. Your mom doesn't really need backup, but you'd still feel better if she had it. You're not totally useless in a fight. Your parents made sure of that: the taser in your backpack isn't ideal against a werewolf, but apply an electrical charge to the testicles, and most anything will feel it.

But Mom will never let you come along, and even if she did, you have another lead to track down, a date with a Kiss-Kiss girl.

It's tempting to storm into school and shakedown every cheerleader you can find, but that way lies truancy write-ups and afternoon detentions; best to wait until after school practice. There will be practice, after all, even though the team's best base just got disemboweled: murder has become commonplace at Kissinger High, and there's a big game tomorrow night. Nothing gets in the way of football in a football town.

If you had a car, you'd park across school and wait; instead, you ride home and sink into the couch. You wish it would eat you. It doesn't. Instead, you blink, and blink again, and then you're back in the church, Laura at your side.

She's wearing her Sunday Best: long sleeves instead of tank tops and cheap jeans without holes in them. Her eyes are yellow instead of blue. Blood still drips from her hair. There's no one else in the church, but you can hear Father Gene's sermon flickering in and out: the wantonness of women, the sin of adultery. What an asshole.

"I'm not what you think," Laura says. It's something she's said before. You'd thought she meant *I'm not the mask I wear*, but you know better now.

"I hate this town."

I don't want to die here.

"You're my only friend who gets it."

You're a timebomb, too, ready to go off.

"I think about a butterflies a lot."

That, you're not so sure how to translate.

She tapes her confession under the pew. "Do you think they remember being caterpillars? Do you think they regret it?"

But you don't want to talk about caterpillars. You have your own confession. "I'm sorry, I'm so sorry I couldn't find you in time."

"But you haven't even started looking. Here. Take this."

It's a scarf, black and glamorous and absurdly long.

There's pink lettering stitched into the silk: *don't let them tame you.*

But then the scarf is wrapped around your throat, choking you and choking you, and when you wake up, it's still there, and Dead Laura is the one tightening the noose, all her insides spilling outside, and that smell, that *smell*—

Until it dissipates and you can move again, breathe again, if too rapidly. Until your dead friend vanishes back into your own head.

Fucking sleep paralysis. Fucking bullshit metaphors.

Practice has already started by the time you get back to Kissinger. You find a good spot, scope out the likely suspects.

Ana Alba, AKA, Double A. 17. Flier. Tiny and vicious. Student Council VP, won on empty campaign promises like gelato vending machines. Serial snapchat cyberbully, and—oh, that's surprising: she's landed badly, falling backwards. She's—

Caught by Veronica Liu. 17. Spotter. One of only two Asian kids in all of KH. Sits to your right in Remedial Math, where she ignores the daily lesson to work on English papers for anyone who will pay. Clever, and clever enough to hide it. Just the kind of girl you try to avoid—although not as much as you avoid Jessica Cassidy, 18, Cheer Captain and bleach-blonde giraffe. Also: Academic Decathlon star, Glee Club washout, and UCLA hopeful—or, at least, determined to land somewhere more prestigious than a state school or local JC. Basically, a mega-bitch, type A on methamphetamines.

You're sure Jessica will scream at Ana for her sloppy landing; instead, she just sighs and calls for a break. The whole team seems out-of-sorts today. Maybe the murders are getting to them, after all. Maybe cheerleaders are more human than you thought.

Five minutes into the break, and you spot it: Ana on the grass, rubbing her ankle, and Veronica palming her something on the sly. Drugs, you think at first, but no: it's a charm bag.

That's good enough for you.

You leave the Kiss-Kiss Girls, wait for Veronica by her ancient deathtrap of a Fiero. It's another forty minutes until she arrives, back in her civvies, hair still wet. She isn't intimidated, of course. Why would she be? She's a witch, and popular, and she's got six inches on you. "Something you wanted, Marceline?"

You don't know the reference. Don't care enough to ask. "Did Laura come to you for a spell?"

That stops her, but only briefly. "What are you—"

"I'm psychic, you're a witch, and my friend was a werewolf, only now she's dead. Can we skip the denial bullshit, please? I need to know why I dreamt about you." She opens her mouth, and you hold up a hand. "Please don't say it's because I'm a lesbian. I am, it's not, and you're smarter than that."

Veronica sighs. "Look, I can guess about the killer, but—"

"Already got that covered. He'll be dead soon enough."

"Good."

There's too much satisfaction in her voice. Is it possible she and Laura were true friends, after all? "Did she come for a spell? Did you meet her at the lake?" Maybe it wasn't witchcraft Laura wanted, but a ride; hard to skip town without one. Did she ask for a lift? Did Veronica show up too late? At all?

Veronica leans against her car, pulls out a Juul. "Sorry," she says, exhaling. "Don't think I can help you."

So much for friends.

You don't have the cash to buy her off, so you lean beside Veronica instead and show her a few pics you took in Remedial Math. "Hate for these to show up in the wrong inbox," you say. "Didn't you just apply for some fancy writing scholarship?"

Veronica tilts her head, lips curled. Helpful, seeing what anger looks like on her face. "Yeah," she says. "All right. Laura needed a spell. Dangerous magic, existentialist shit. She said it was her only way out. Looked like she meant it, so I helped."

You snort. "And how much did that cost?"

"As much as she had," Veronica says, matter of fact. "Dangerous magic isn't cheap, and even fancy writing scholarships aren't full rides."

She has a point, but you're either too exhausted or too petty to concede it. "What was the spell?"

"The anima bisection," Veronica says. "I don't know; I didn't name it. Some old auntie must've really been into Jung. Anyway, it's not something most people survive. Can't be a stock character."

A normal person, she means. "What does it do?"

"What it sounds like: it splits your essence in half."

"Like…a Horcrux?"

Her lips twitch. "More like Dr. Jekyll and Mr. Hyde. You read that in DeWitt's class yet?"

Well. You got assigned it, anyway. "I know the basics."

"Right. Look, it's not a split between good and evil. Not even id and ego, more like…your past self and some possibility hiding inside you. Between the wild—"

"And the tamed."

Veronica exhales. Her smoke rings look more like wormholes. "Whatever half you lose," she says, "you lose for good."

You think about that.

You think about those strange claw marks, all that inside-out meat: torn apart, obviously, but from outside or from within?

You think about Laura, who couldn't be perfect anymore. Laura, who had something dangerous and reckless living inside, Laura, who wanted to live, who couldn't wait, who knew you wouldn't follow. Couldn't, for more reasons than one.

You think about the memories of butterflies, and of all their left-behind caterpillar friends.

"You understand now," Veronica says. "Don't you? You get what really happened?"

There's a very fine tremor in her fingers. You didn't notice it before, but some lingering signs of trauma are understandable. She was at the lake. She saw it all.

Laura was right. In the end, you do understand why she

did it.

"I get it," you say. "I know how to find her now."

It may require a mask and bolt-cutters and tasing some hapless Animal Control officer, but eventually, you sneak the wolf out of the impound and into the passenger seat of Veronica's car. She helpfully loaned it to you, after you deleted any incriminating photos from the Cloud.

You drive to the edge of the woods, open the door. The wolf quickly jumps, making a beeline for the trees, before stopping and looking back at you.

Her eyes are yellow, fierce and unforgiving.

"We could still leave it all behind," you tell her. Your voice is scraped raw. "We can take Veronica's car; go anywhere we want. Be anything we want."

But that was always a pipedream, wasn't it, one that belonged to the Laura who died in the lake. Whatever's left of her now has dreams of her own, and they're not yours to share.

You did what she needed. You found her. But you knew from the start: you would always be too late.

You never had time to save the Laura that loved you.

She blinks at you once, twice, then turns away and disappears into the woods.

You go home.

No one's there. You order pizza, take a bite, and immediately start crying. Who knows why. Laura didn't even like pizza.

You cry until you fall asleep.

It's the church again. No one else is inside, but you can hear Laura's howls flickering in and out. Hopefully, she ate Father Gene.

There's another letter taped under the pew.

You could be a butterfly too, it says, *if you wanted.*

But Laura isn't a butterfly. She's a caterpillar who cut herself in half to survive. And maybe that would keep you from imploding, too; maybe you could buy the spell off Veronica, somehow, save yourself. Shed this sense of suffocating responsibility, this skin of obedient daughter, of teenage girl, and embrace whatever wondrous possibility hides inside you. Maybe you could be some wandering spark, pure investigative inspiration: a muse that loves briefly, then moves on. Always the one who leaves first, and is never left behind.

But that makes your parents dead caterpillars, doesn't it, in this bullshit metaphor? You still can't stand for that, and anyway, you don't want to be half a thing.

You turn the paper over. *I can be wild,* you write, *without being killed by my own scarves.*

Your phone wakes you up. Coordinates. Your mom has finished the hunt. You grab her a change of clothes and bike back to the fucking woods.

She's covered in blood, of course, eyes still black. There are two corpses at her feet: Jake and Sheriff-Coroner Valento. Jake died mid-shift. They both died screaming. Their skin hangs off their bones, like ribbons.

You nod at Valento. "Human?"

"Only technically."

More human than your mom, then. The kind of monster who covers up his son's murders, time and again. Not the kind desperate to avenge her own son—Kyle Abbott, 14, skipped-a-grade-smart and helplessly goofy—not the kind who sings her eight-year-old daughter to sleep, then sneaks out to the crossroads and agrees to house a devil. More human than your dad too, who's always been drawn to the dark and lonely places, who found the Old Ones cultists, piece by bloody piece, and helped your mom bury them, rather than locking her away.

More human than you too, maybe, as you pick up a shovel and casually bury what's left. Split apart or stitched together, that's always been the person you are: you'll bury or blackmail anyone in order to survive, to follow the clues, to help your family, to save what's left of a friend.

But you can't stay caged anymore. You have to open your mouth.

You wait until your dad is released, until you're all back home, celebrating with milkshakes. You say, "I love you both, just so goddamn much, but put me in the game, or I walk."

MONSTERS NEVER LEAVE YOU

MONSTERS NEVER LEAVE YOU

SOMETHING KNOCKS ON the door[1]. Esther, dreaming, would like to ignore it. Instead, she blinks awake and grabs her shotgun, because dead things typically call for bullets, not spell work, and whatever wants inside her home is certainly dead.

In retrospect, she should've expected the children.

The boy's feet are stained with grave dirt and tree bark. The girl's feet are stained with bone dust and blood. They're weak and exhausted and tightly holding each other's hands. Only one of them is alive in the traditional sense.

"Well," Esther says, lowering her shotgun. "Best come in, then. We'll get you cocoa."

The children are witches. Neither give their names.

The boy has pale blue eyes, icy white skin, and a mouth

---

1. Child murder, violence, miscarriage, death of parent, imprisonment, child abuse, parental neglect, child abandonment, cannibalism.

so red she'd assumed it was bleeding. He takes cinnamon with his cocoa. His sister, meanwhile, must favor whipped cream: Esther pours a towering dollop straight from the kitchen faucet.

House knows everyone's favorites, children most of all.

The girl stares at the kitchen table. "We followed the birds," she says, not touching her mug. "They led us to you."

Birds. Esther would shoot every one of them out of the sky, given enough time and ammunition. "Things with wings are tricky. You'll need to be careful, listening to their advice."

The boy leans forward eagerly. There's something about him Esther doesn't know how to read, something underneath his skin, like bark wrapped around his fingerbones. Neither witchery nor death can account for it. "So, you really—you hear them, too?"

The girl swallows. "M—m-mother said the Devil …"

Oh. They had *that* kind of mother.

"If there is a Devil," Esther tells them firmly, "he has nothing to do with us. It's important you understand that. Witchcraft isn't what you think."

"What is it, then? M-mother said, but she was, she …"

Esther waits.

The girl looks up, eyes large and dark and full of confession. "She wasn't very good."

Esther's own mother hadn't been very good, either— and her father, little better. Parents are a lingering infection, an ugly wound that only pretends to heal. "Well," she says, running a spoon through her own spire of whipped cream.

"Magic isn't absolute power or a nonconsensual exchange. It's not a *taking*. There's no perversion of the natural order—"

"But," the boy interrupts, "I'm dead."

Esther eyes the jagged scars looping around his neck.

"Somewhat," she admits. "But your sister called your bones, and your bones agreed to rise. Your sister needed you, so you came back. What could be more natural than that?"

The girl's mouth is a flat, unimpressed line. Esther can't blame her: resurrection and reconstitution are very powerful magics, especially for a child twenty-five year's Esther's junior. Even she hadn't been so powerful at that age—deadly, yes, but those aren't always the same thing.

She tries not to think about that. It doesn't do to dwell.

You're living in the wrong house, her mind whispers, if you're still trying to move on.

She dismisses Peter's voice with practiced ease. It's easy to do when he isn't here to relentlessly repeat the same advice like a sanctimonious parrot.

"How …" The girl looks away. "How did you know that —that *I* brought him—"

"Feet tell stories," Esther says. "Best we wash them now."

She grabs warm washcloths, as well as bandages for the girl, whose skin has bled badly during the long journey through the woods. The two siblings look little alike: the girl is rosy where her brother is ghostly, and chubby where the boy is frail. But when she lifts their feet to clean them, Esther sees what only a witch could see: the same blue staining their heels, the bitter juice of juniper berries.

"Well," Esther says. "That explains a few things."

Their story comes out in pieces over the next few weeks.

"I've always been strange," Kit says one night, poking at the pink snowmen that Millie had spun from House's cotton candy insulation. The girl is asleep now, and her name isn't actually Millie, any more than the boy is Kit. But Esther doesn't press; names are a strange magic, and she hadn't been born Esther, herself. "Even before I was dead, I was wrong."

"Different," she corrects. "Never wrong. Your mother—"

"Millie's mother. She. She didn't like me much."

He rubs absently at his throat.

Ah, Esther thinks, and says nothing.

The woman's dead, though, Esther is almost sure, and the kind of dead that stays silent and still in the ground. Had Millie killed her? Had Kit? Something else, still looking for them?

"How are you different?" Esther asks instead. "How does your witching manifest?"

Kit shrugs. "I just talk to things. And things talk back. They make a lot more sense than people."

"Like birds?"

"Birds, stones, rivers." He hesitates. "Trees."

"Trees?"

Kit stays quiet.

"How about houses?" Esther asks. "Can you hear this one?"

The boy brightens. "I like House. They're nice. Some houses don't like me, but most schools do. Churches, too."

Esther has no particular affinity for churches. They mean well, perhaps, but her ears have never caught more than the faintest whispers, quiet hallelujahs wafting through air that smells of copper and salt. And since…well. She hasn't been able to face a church in years.

Homes are different, though: attics long to tell her their stories, while kitchens stretch to suit her needs and libraries nudge books in her direction. To be a witch is to be haunted, every spell a conversation, every day a new ghost story.

"And Millie?" Esther asks.

Kit scrunches his nose. "She likes *people*, couldn't hear anything else. But she wanted to learn, so I tried to teach her. I don't think I did it right."

It's surprising he did it at all; most folk are witches, or they're not. But exceptions do happen. Peter, for instance.

"Millie got these fancy plates to listen; they were flying everywhere, but then …" Kit shivers. "*She* saw. The way she looked, when she asked, 'Don't you want, don't you want …'"

His hand returns to his scars.

Esther has little experience with this. People find her in these woods, of course, mostly lost children, sometimes a cursed woman seeking aid, but none of them have ever been murdered before. She tries to think of something comforting—

—But then, Millie screams.

Esther and Kit find her downstairs this time, stumbling out the front door. They follow her outside to the ancient and gargantuan redwood nearby. Millie is awake but unaware, clammy, horror-struck. "Sap," she says, kneeling, as Kit wraps his cold little arms around his sister and Esther sinks down, rocking them both. "It, it slid out of her, with the blood and the baby, and then the branches, they burst—"

"Shhh," Esther says.

Millie's eyes are blank. "Her belly. Her fingernails. You didn't see the *roots*."

These aren't Millie's words. These aren't her memories; her witching, so weak in the daylight, seems to come alive with the moon. Millie dreams other people's secrets. Esther isn't sure who this one belongs to.

Nibble, nibble, little mouse, Millie had whispered just the other night. Who is nibbling at my house?

Decades later, Esther's breath still catches at those words.

Now she hushes, shushes, and soothes until Millie fully comes back to herself. She doesn't seem ready to stand, so Esther introduces them to the redwood. Its leaves rustle in the wind, a fond *hello, little ones*.

"Redwoods are powerful beings," Esther says. "Cranky, yes, but they give excellent advice. Trees are like witches: each has their own magic. Be mindful of that when you cast. It's very rude to call on something that can't offer what you seek."

It's Kit who finally asks, "What magic do juniper trees have?"

The wind picks up. The redwood shudders. The birds and the bugs go silent.

"Vengeance," Esther says. "Violence. Juniper trees are creatures of crossroads and war, and they don't take kindly to impertinence or maltreatment." She thinks of Millie's nightmare, of branches bursting through bellies. Someone must have been impertinent, indeed. "It's the first rule of witchcraft, the most important: you always ask. You never take."

It's the rule, she doesn't add, that so many witches break.

They go inside. House is awake, of course, eager to provide warmth and brown sugar solace—but as Esther crosses into the kitchen, three spoons fall to the floor.

"Damn," she whispers.

"Esther?"

Esther's bones ache, heavy with the weight of prophecy, of exhausting inevitability. She thought she'd have more time.

"Company's coming," she tells the children, and throws the spoons in the sink.

The first visitor arrives the next night.

It's the witching hour. Millie and Kit sit at the kitchen table, both shaken from the girl's latest dream. *Don't you want an apple?* she'd whispered, staring sightlessly at her brother. *Don't you want an apple? They're in the trunk.*

House, anxiously shifting at the children's distress, oozes lines of chocolate and raspberry from their walls.

Esther scowls at this latest, dripping decor. "Witchcraft isn't …?"

"A perversion of the natural order," Kit and Millie say.

"Yes. Witchcraft is a way to communicate with that order: it's asking impossible fruit to grow, or faces to change, or houses to stop creating cavities they don't have to pay for."

Peanut butter begins seeping too, insolently.

"That's unsanitary," Esther tells House, but waves a relenting hand. Kit attacks the raspberry; being dead has had little effect on his appetite. Millie kneels down and uncertainly prods the peanut butter.

"The house doesn't listen to you," she says.

"House always listens. They just don't always agree. Their whole purpose is to spoil children. That's what they were built for. In a way."

House anxiously shifts again. Bourbon caramel this time, her favorite.

Esther smiles fondly. "It's all right. That's been over a long while now."

Millie frowns. "What's wrong? Is the house—"

Someone knocks on the door.

It's familiar, insistent, the impatient rap of a policeman. It speaks of authority, among other things.

"It's okay," Esther tells the children. "You're safe."

She grabs the shotgun anyway before opening the door.

Peter stands there, bony arms crossed tight across his chest. "Dramatic," he says dryly.

"You're the one prowling the woods in the middle of the night. Couldn't sleep?"

He laughs, almost. "Sleep? Do people still do that?"

"You know people better than me."

"Well, if you'd just—" Peter cuts himself off, sighing. "You gonna let me in?"

"Why don't you ask House?"

He rocks back slightly, jaw tightening. "You have the kids," he says finally. It's not a question: Peter can read footprints and faces the way she can read hands and feet. He can find just about anyone, has been chasing down people since he was fifteen. How would their lives have gone, if she hadn't listened to those fucking birds?

But then, she wouldn't have House.

"They don't belong here," Peter says. "You don't, either."

Esther sighs and beckons him inside.

Kit's in the kitchen doorway, standing protectively in front of his sister. Millie's crouched down behind him, peeking out carefully, a paring knife in one hand. "It's okay," Esther says. "This is my brother, Peter. He's very tiresome, but he won't hurt you."

Still, she doesn't let go of the shotgun.

Peter says hello, smiling kindly; neither child responds to it. He doesn't push, though; he's good with people. Ought to be, considering how many he's taken from her— but that's unfair. Esther helped House reshape their purpose: no longer a lure, but a waystation, a safe harbor for the lost, the seeking, the desperate. People aren't meant to stay forever.

Only Esther.

She ushers the children back to the table, gives them bowls of feathers and buttons and paper birds. "Ask them to float, see if they'll agree. We'll be in the other room if you need us."

In the other room, Peter hands her a case file.

"Your strays are missing persons in a murder investigation. One woman is dead. Her body ..."

Her body has been impaled on the branch of a juniper tree. Mouth open, skin grey. Wood splinters burst from her left eye. Esther can't tell much from her feet—the angle is wrong—but she can see they're covered in blood. It's dripping from her toes: down, down, down into a hole in the ground beneath her.

Something had been buried in that hole, something that had clawed its way back up.

"My guys think it's the husband," Peter says, "but his face isn't right for it."

Esther examines the woman again. Dark hair, high cheekbones. A thin, hooked nose. Millie looks just like her.

"The boy—" Peter says.

Esther may not be able to read faces like her brother, but she can guess. "Grave dirt on his cheeks?"

"And a jawbone made of wood." Peter shakes his head, wondering. "I've never seen a face like it. It's not just the resurrection, is it? He was born different."

Sap, it slid out of her, with the blood and the baby ...

Esther crosses her arms. "He didn't kill her."

"Do you really know that?"

"No," Esther admits. "But I know she killed him first."

Peter winces. "I hoped I was wrong. It's harder to read the dead than the living, but…there was abuse. Not sexual, but emotional and physical. We found a trunk in the cellar. There was blood inside, and on the rim, too."

Don't you want an apple?

Esther can see Kit there, kneeling over the trunk. She can imagine his stepmother behind him, hands on the lid. Kit's scars wrap around his entire throat. How many times would it have taken before the woman—before Kit's *head*—

Esther rubs the back of her neck. "And the father?"

"He didn't know."

Didn't know? Or didn't want to see?

There are people who are afraid to leave, fearing only worse harm will come; people trying to break through years of psychological conditioning, of financial dependency. Parents terrified their babies will be taken away. And then there are those other people who close their eyes because they can, who convince themselves not to intervene, who never wanted the burden of responsibility in the first place.

"He's sorry," Peter says, but Esther isn't sure which shitty father he's apologizing for.

"Right," she says, turning away.

"Goddamn it, Esther, can't you just once—"

"Forgiveness has to be earned—"

"You never let him earn it! You never even tried to understand—"

"*Understand*?" Esther whirls around. "Jesus, Peter, how broken are you?"

"Me? You ran away to hide in the woods for twenty years! You're living in the house that tried to *eat us*—"

"Esther?"

The children hover nervously in the archway. House—oh, House is trembling hard.

"It's okay," she says, to everyone. "We were just..."

She looks to Peter for help. Even now, she still does that.

"We argue sometimes," he says softly, keeping his hands where the children can see them. "But we don't hurt each other."

Not anymore, he doesn't say.

"That's right," Esther agrees. "And Peter, he's come to take you back to town, if you like."

Immediately, the siblings step back.

"You're not in any trouble," Peter says. "I don't need to know exactly what happened that night. But this, this is no place for children."

House trembles harder.

Peter pretends he doesn't feel it as he takes back his file, papers clenched between his fingers. "You should be in school with other kids, with parents who take care of you—"

"*Our* parents didn't take care of us," Kit says.

Peter nods. "I know. I'm sorry. But your stepmother can't hurt you anymore, and your father's in custody right now. If he gets released, if it's safe, you could be together again."

Millie looks up. Kit doesn't.

"Where would we go now?" Millie asks.

"We'd find a family to place you with," Peter says. "A

good family. I'd make sure."

He would, too. That, at least, Esther can count on.

"A witch family?" Kit asks, still turned away.

Peter hesitates. "I don't know."

Millie shakes her head. "No," she says, as Kit slumps in relief. "No, I don't want to go. Esther, can't we stay?"

Yes, Esther thinks, but you'll change your mind eventually.

"Yes," she says. "If that's what you both want."

For now, at least, it is.

She escorts Peter outside. His shoulders are hunched, too much salt in his hair. He needs to eat more, like always.

"Peter. You know it was never House."

He nods, eyes distant. "Some things are hard to separate."

Truer words, Esther thinks, watching him.

"Esther? I'm so—"

"I know," she says, because he's said it before, a hundred times over. "I forgive you."

And it's true. She forgave him a long time ago. She's always understood. But—

"But you don't trust me," Peter says.

She doesn't want to lie to him. Can't, because the shotgun is still in her hands. "I love you."

"Yeah," Peter says, smiling sadly. "I love you, too."

"But you can't forgive me," Esther says.

Peter must not want to lie to her, either, because he just shakes his head and walks away.

The next day, Kit, Millie, and House surprise her with pancakes. They all sit in bed, eating and continuing their abandoned levitation exercises. Millie has no luck until Esther remembers the handful of chicken bones she'd been saving for a shielding potion; then, they swirl easily through the air. Bone speaks freely to Millie, no matter the time of day.

Occasionally, the children glance at each other, unsubtly.

"House was sad yesterday—" Kit finally begins, only for Millie to poke him in the arm.

"*Esther* was sad!"

"I *know* that!"

"It's not just things that matter! People—"

"House isn't just a *thing*—"

"We were both sad," Esther interrupts, before their bickering escalates. "Peter brings up difficult memories."

Kit crosses his arms. "House doesn't like him."

"Peter's not very fond of House, himself."

"*I* don't like him. House says he hurt you."

"And has House ever hurt anybody?"

Kit frowns, uncertain. House stays very quiet.

"People haven't been kind to you," Esther says. "It's easier, sometimes, trusting things without mouths. But you don't need a mouth to lie to someone, and it's not just people who make terrible mistakes."

"You're saying...House is bad?"

"Not at all. But truth isn't objective. Everyone has their own."

The children stare blankly.

Esther sighs. "When we were young," she says, "our

parents abandoned us in these woods. Mother's idea, but Father went along with it. There wasn't enough food, you see. Children get so hungry. But I could follow the birds, and this place was like a dream, a house we could eat. Only the witch who built it was hungry, too, and her appetites were…unusual. Mad."

"What did she eat?" Kit asks.

"Children."

Millie, suddenly pale, jumps up and is noisily sick in the bathroom. Kit won't meet Esther's eyes.

"I'm sorry," she says, confused, when the girl returns. Esther's past is a horror show, and Millie's the more sensitive of the two, but to have a visceral reaction like that …

"It's o-o-o—" Millie squeezes her eyes shut. "Keep going."

Esther does, reluctantly. "The witch was House's mother, and they loved her dearly. But House didn't like hurting children. So, when the witch asked—"

"House said no," Kit says.

"Yes."

"But she broke the rule, anyway."

"Repeatedly. A lot of witches do. Bad witches always rely on luck, demanding whatever they want from weaker, vulnerable things. They're certain they'll have the upper hand because they've always had it before. But eventually, luck must turn."

"What happened to the bad witch?" Millie whispers.

Please be bigger, be hotter. Please don't let her out.

"She died," Esther says.

Kit crosses his arms again, mulish. "So, House helped you."

"Yes. And I forgave House. I love them very much."

"Then Peter should forgive House, too. It's been fifty years!"

"I'm not *that* old," Esther says dryly. "And forgiveness can't come with a clock. You ask. You never demand."

"But—"

Very gently, Esther reaches out and touches the boy's jagged scars. "Would you forgive the trunk?" she asks. "Would you feel safe, leaning over it again?"

Kit begins to cry. He runs and Millie runs after him, leaving Esther alone with a handful of crumpled paper birds. And House, but House is still too quiet, lost somewhere in their own memories. Everything smells faintly of black licorice.

No one here likes black licorice. No one alive, anyway.

"It's okay," she tells House, "if you still love her. Parents are…we can talk about it."

But House says nothing.

The second visitor comes on the full moon.

It's been a tense few days. Kit has barely said a word to anyone, only murmuring his secrets to the rocks. Now he's pretending to read as Millie huddles near Esther on the bed, clammy and desperate. These memories, for once, are Millie's own.

"He was all pieces," she whispers. "First his head,

rolling. M—m-mother said I pushed him t-too hard. And I believed her, I thought that I'd—that I'd—and then. In the kitchen, into the pots and pans, so many pieces—"

"You're safe now," Esther says. "You're both safe."

"He ate him. Daddy ate him all up."

"Shhh—"

"It's because of me. M-mother had to save me; I had the Devil in me now, but I asked Kit for it, I asked for the Devil. Kit, because of me—"

"There's no Devil, sweetheart—"

And then bone against oak, the sound echoing in Esther's ribcage: once, twice, thrice.

There's no Devil, but the living don't knock like that.

It's too much to hope that there's a dead brother the children have forgotten to mention. Esther tells them to stay, then grabs her shotgun to meet the corpse from Peter's file.

But it's not Millie's mother at the door.

The dead woman wears a torn, dirty sundress. Underneath it, her belly is huge and pale; twisted branches grow from it, angling in all directions. Tree roots have burst from underneath her fingernails, and spill out the corners of her eyes.

Oh, Millie. Sweetheart, why didn't you tell me you called more than you meant to?

Esther looks at the woman's fleshless feet, sculpted only from bark and bone. "You're Kit's mother."

"Deborah," the woman agrees. Her voice is the hushed wind between trees. "Or I was. I've been in the ground too long. We're different now. We think together. Rooted."

"We?"

Deborah blinks slowly. "It needed an acolyte."

Juniper trees are creatures of crossroads and war, Esther remembers, dazed. If you can't come to the crossroads …

Well. It's not like she's never spoken with trees before. This one just borrows human skin, and feasts on the bones and blood of murderers and fools.

Esther grips her shotgun tighter.

"If you've come for food," she says carefully, "you'll find none here. I wish you luck on your hunt, but I'm not interested in being a sacrifice, and the children are not yours to eat."

Deborah laughs, or the juniper tree does. "I seldom eat children unless they've been rude, and the boy was always kind. He is of my fruit. I would like him back."

"Of your …?"

The tree-witch holds out her palm.

Her life line has been cut in half, literally. Within the wound, Esther can see blood drops, and snow, and small teeth biting into anomalous blue fruit. "I needed the fruit to bear a child," Deborah says. It must be Deborah speaking now. "I needed a tree to bear the fruit. It told me—I told her —it wasn't made for that kind of magic, but I wanted what I wanted. I wouldn't take no for an answer."

Fool, indeed.

Esther eyes Deborah's hands: motionless, content. "Do you even want what you died for? Are you here for a servant or son?"

"We all serve something. I find pleasure in my purpose. He will, too, likely."

"Likely?"

The tree-witch shrugs.

"And Millie?"

"She's done me a service, raised me an acolyte. But she can't hear my words, and has no stomach for the work."

Esther thinks of Millie's mother, impaled, blood dripping into an empty grave. Millie, she thinks, has an iron stomach, considering the things she's seen—

I asked for the Devil.

—and the things she blames herself for.

"It's been centuries," the juniper tree whispers, "since I've had anyone to bring me the wicked and delicious."

"They're children," Esther says. "They deserve a family."

"Is that what you think you're giving them, here, in this lonely candy house?"

Despite herself, Esther's throat locks up.

"You look at us and see a monster," the tree-witch says. "But was it monsters or humans who hurt you most? Monsters never left you. Monsters didn't hurt that boy upstairs, didn't beat him down with the Word of God. The trees never ignored his bruises. Witches didn't take his head. Even the girl was failed by her people: too fat, too anxious and teary. What has the world ever done for them?" Deborah steps closer as gingerbread roof tiles clatter to the ground. "Give them to us. Maybe she'll grow into an exceptional monster, after all."

But the children aren't hers to give.

"Not your call," Esther says, and points the shotgun at Deborah's face. Deborah smiles, her mouth wide—

"No, thank you."

Esther tenses. For witches, the children are very poor listeners.

Kit stands beside her. "Your invitation is kind," he says, "but I already chose Millie. I will always choose Millie."

"She can come—"

"No," Millie says, too quickly. "I choose Esther."

The words burn. She pushes the pain down.

"We'll bid you a safe journey, then," Esther says, but Deborah—and it must be Deborah, still impertinent even in death—crosses the threshold anyway.

"You can't stop us," she says, reaching with one gnarled hand, right before her shin bone cracks in half.

Millie steps forward, one fist raised in the air.

"Your bones like me more than they like you," she says.

The hand retracts. Slowly, the tree in the woman straightens. "Our apologies," she says, stepping backwards on a leg that barely holds her. "The choice was made."

"Don't ask it again," Esther says, and slams the door shut.

Dawn finds Esther exhausted, sick of bedsheets that tease her with sleep. She gets up, finds Millie scowling ferociously at Esther's grimoire. Studying potions is a good idea for the girl—memorized ingredients will work as well as instinctual ones, provided they're agreeable enough—but whatever is inside this cauldron smells...inauspicious.

Millie's cheeks burn. "I wanted a forgiveness potion."

"That's...not really a thing," Esther says eventually. This particular elixir is for meditation, clarity of thought—things that could lead towards forgiveness, or warn against it. "Is this for you to drink, or someone else?"

Millie is silent. Maybe she doesn't even know herself.

"Sweetheart. The things your mother did, that Kit's mother did, they aren't your fault. Never let other people blame you for their choices."

"But I made choices, too! I made them, and then Kit was dead, and M-mother was dead, and D-d-da-d—"

Millie shoves the cauldron off the stovetop.

Esther winces at the resounding crack of iron violently meeting wood. Green spills everywhere and House drops the temperature in indignation. At least the cauldron was barely warm. "Okay, let's just—"

Millie presses a shaking fist to her mouth. "I'm sorry," she says. "I'm sorry, I'm, I'm, I'm—"

"It's okay, Millie—"

"I'm mad at him."

Esther frowns. "Kit?"

Millie shakes her head. "I'm mad at him," she repeats, "but you said everyone makes mistakes. The house made a mistake, but you love them anyway, right? You forgave them 'cause you love them?"

"Millie—"

"He'll forgive me, I think. I dreamt he would. Shouldn't I forgive him, too?"

Esther is definitely the wrong person to ask about forgiveness. She opens her mouth, and does nothing with it.

Millie turns away. "I'm sorry. I'll clean it all up."

Esther hesitates. "Okay," she says finally. "Then we can work on your potion together. Does that sound good?"

Millie hums, refusing to look up.

Esther sighs and, leaving Millie with a handful of dishrags, steps outside for a moment alone to regroup. Only Kit's awake, too, sitting beside the bellflowers. Shyly, they emerge under his cold, welcoming hands.

"Hey," Esther says, sitting next to him.

"Have you ever been dead?" Kit asks.

She should've stayed inside with Millie. "No," Esther admits.

Kit nods. "I didn't like it," he says, after a while.

Esther has to take a breath. "I'm glad you came back," she says eventually.

"Me too," Kit says. He glances over, pale eyes wide with wanting. "I like it here. I like it."

But she can hear what he isn't saying.

I will always choose Millie.

"I understand," Esther says. "I made that choice too, once. Chose Peter until the day I had to choose myself."

Kit frowns. "You're saying I shouldn't—"

"No. No, I'd never say that. Just …"

Esther tries not to think of the church cellar. Tries not to think of Peter's face, before he'd locked the door.

"If there comes a day," Esther says, "when you can't choose Millie, or when she can't choose you…you have to let go."

Kit frowns harder. "I don't understand."

"I know," Esther says sadly. "I know."

The third visitor comes at dusk, and he doesn't come alone.

Esther is teaching the children their times tables—it can't always be magic, sadly—when the knock comes. It's wet with something, sweat, maybe. Living, anxious, redemptive flesh.

She doesn't want to answer the door.

But she is Esther, and House is House, and they will always, always open the door for a stranger seeking something they lost. Even if what they lost is something they gave up.

She grabs her shotgun to meet who's come.

He's white, in his thirties, wearing a crisp polo shirt at odds with his dark stubble and haunted eyes. The things he's seen—the deaths of his wives, the resurrection of his son—are still shaking his bones. He looks at his children and shakes harder.

Kit and Millie, Esther decides, favor their dead mothers.

"You brought him, then," Esther says to Peter, who's standing off to the side, fidgeting.

"He never would've found his way alone."

He would've, if he tried hard enough. It might have taken years, but he would have. "How helpful of you," Esther says. "Like a tour guide. Like a bird."

Peter looks up, hurt etched into his white knuckles. "Do you only care about choices when you're the one making them?"

It hits Esther in the lungs, the way it was meant to. She

inclines her head and steps back, but the man makes no move to step inside, just stares hopelessly at his children.

"Marlene—"

"Millie," Millie says, arms crossed and lips trembling. "I'm Millie now. And—"

"He doesn't need to call me anything," Kit interrupts. "He never bothered before."

The man sinks to his knees. "I'm so sorry. I, I should have paid more attention, should've realized how much she —I'm so glad you're okay—"

"Okay?" Kit asks tonelessly. "She killed me. She killed me, and you ate me, and my sister gathered up my bones, buried me under the juniper tree, and you think—"

"No, no, of course not, but I didn't, I never knew—"

"You knew enough. You knew how she treated me; you knew what she said. But you never did anything. You never looked at me and saw anything but the juniper tree." Kit tilts his head. "That's how you're looking at me now."

"I'm—"

"If I scared you before when I was just a witch, how are you going to deal with me now that I'm dead?"

The man, shaking harder, can't meet his son's eyes. He turns to Millie, with her normal mouth and smooth, unscarred neck. "I love you. You know that, right? I made mistakes, terrible mistakes, but I love you."

"You left us, Daddy."

"I—"

"Kit crawled out of the ground," Millie says, "and his mom did too, and M-mother, she dragged Mother to the tree, *she dragged Mother to the tree*, and you *left us*."

94

The man covers his face. "Terrible mistakes," he whispers.

Esther and Peter look at each other.

It'll be different now, Father swears in her memory. It was your mother, all her idea; I should never have listened —but, but she's gone now. It'll be different, you'll see.

But it had been too different; that was the problem. Esther could never forget Father had abandoned them. Peter could never forget the witch's face. He was terrified, and she was furious, and they were both traumatized, sparking with magic. They were too strange, too difficult, and one day, too much. One day, they'd woken up to a note in their father's place.

It's better for everyone this way.

"It'll be different," the man says, as Millie inches forward, as Kit slumps. He must suspect what Esther has known for years: fathers who leave only come back to disappoint you. But Peter, he'd needed to believe so badly. Even after the note, he'd been so desperate to believe.

I'll find him; I can do it. He's just upset. I won't be any trouble this time, though. I'll do better. I'll be good.

Peter, Esther is startled to realize, is crying.

Millie is, too. "Daddy," she says, stepping towards him—

But Peter's there, suddenly, kneeling between them.

"Don't," he begs Millie. "I was wrong before. I'm always wrong. Don't make my mistakes."

"Peter—"

"Hey, you can't—"

Peter ignores them. "If you're ready to forgive," he says,

"then forgive. But don't do it just because you love someone. Love is a gift, not an obligation."

He does turn, then, meets Esther's eyes. "Choose them if they're right for you."

Esther can't speak.

The man in the doorway stands. "This place isn't your home," he says—but only to Millie, always to Millie. "I know you never wanted any of this. We'll find a new house, somewhere far away. Put all this misery behind us. You can be normal again, I know it. We'll be happy again. Marlene—"

But Millie steps back, squeezes Kit's hand.

"I'm Millie now," she repeats.

"Baby—"

"We choose Esther," Kit says, cutting him off.

The words burn, but only because no one's ever said them before and meant it.

Later, much later, there's a knock on the door.

The children are in bed, no nightmares yet. No telling how long that will last. Esther glances at her shotgun, leaves it where it is. Sits beside Peter on the stoop.

The siderails, usually chocolate, are now cinnamon sticks. Peter's favorite.

He reaches out, wondering…and then shudders and pulls back, bony arms wrapping tightly around his stomach.

It still feels like such a step.

"Thank you," Esther says.

"Don't thank—"

"Thank you."

Peter shrugs, eyes on the trees. "I owe you. More than I can ever give."

"I owe you, too—"

"No," Peter says, shaking his head. "You saved my life. You saved me, and I repaid you by locking you up—"

I'm sorry, I can't let you go. It's just till I find Father, I swear; it'll be better. I swear, I'm so sorry—

"I told you," Esther says unsteadily. "I forgave you for that—"

"The church cellar didn't like it," Peter pushes on, breathlessly. "It wasn't that kind of church; it wanted to welcome people, not imprison them. But you couldn't hear churches, so I broke the rule. I locked you in, just like—"

"Peter," Esther says, more firmly.

"I just didn't want you to leave me. And I couldn't come back here; you *knew* I couldn't come back here—"

She had, and that decision still haunts her, even if it'd been the one she'd needed to make. Esther couldn't keep chasing their father. She couldn't keep hoping that he'd change, that he'd remember love was meant to be unconditional. She wasn't the daughter he wanted. She wouldn't apologize for it, not ever again. Esther had needed to figure out who she was, who she could be; she'd needed to come back and face what had happened—but Peter hadn't been ready, and she'd known that. She'd made it impossible for him to choose her.

She'd known he'd be upset, maybe even furious, but she

hadn't expected his devastation, his sheer panic. She'd never thought—

She was in that cellar for days before she finally escaped.

"I was so scared of being alone," Peter whispers. "I was so scared all the time, and I kept telling myself, I had to be stronger, I could hold us together, if I could just bring him back, if I could just make you both *see*—"

Esther takes his hand. "I know, Peter."

"I was the one who couldn't see. I stole your choice. You shouldn't trust me."

"But I do," Esther says, and it isn't a lie, not entirely.

He looks at her.

She ignores her own tears. "Some things are hard to separate," she admits, and he smiles softly at that. "Anyway, it's better today than yesterday. Isn't it?"

He nods. "I know you didn't do anything wrong. You don't need forgiveness, but I do forgive you, I should, I almost—"

Peter reaches out towards House again, this time making fingerprints in the cinnamon.

Esther's tired of dwelling. She's so damn tired of memories, of letting mistrust choose for her again and again.

"Come back tomorrow," she asks him. "We'll have dinner."

And Peter says quietly, "Okay."

———————————

15 Eulogies Scribbled Inside a Hello Kitty Notebook

15 EULOGIES SCRIBBLED INSIDE A HELLO KITTY NOTEBOOK

February—Liam

I didn't know him well[1]. Nobody did, really: he was the new kid. But he was funny, and he was cute, and I probably would've said yes when he asked me out, except that's when the gullet-eaters attacked, and he didn't know not to scream. Stuff like gullet-eaters and werewolves and carnivorous pixies didn't happen at his old school, I guess. Anyway, they ripped his throat out in seconds. Pulled out his esophagus. Chewed. His body twitched for a long time, arterial spray everywhere. It was a Tuesday, probably.

I think about Liam often, or at least whenever I study physics. The library couldn't replace my blood-spattered textbook. Budget cuts, you know.

---

1. violence, suicidal thought/ideation, implied parental death, gore, suicide.

February—Mr. Morales

Listen. Some teachers inspire you, lift you up. Other hold you back, think you're worthless. And then you've got teachers like Mr. Morales, who never gave a shit what you did, so long as you were quiet about it, and put on movies like *It's a Wonderful Life* when he didn't feel like teaching anymore. I liked him, or I understood him. I mean, we're all just trying to get through the day, right?

But eventually, Morales didn't get through the day. They found his body in a supply closet, completely drained of blood, and Economics suddenly became Civics & Economics, leaving poor Mrs. Bradley with 63 students to teach while the vice principal probably sacrificed a small goat just to summon a substitute who'd actually stick out a full day.

Morales stuck it out whole decades, though. I guess that counts for something.

March—Olive

Look, I'm just going to say it. Olive was a dick. She thought she was the smartest kid in class, and who knows, maybe she was right, but also? An absolute DICK. Never met another girl with such fucking mansplainer energy. Hand up in every class. Condescending smile. *Well, ACTUALLY.* Shut the fuck up, you bleach-blonde pitted fruit, you're not gonna make it to Stanford, no one makes it out of this town, no one makes it out alive. I mean, fuck. I'm sorry, I'm sorry for her mom and her sisters and all, but I don't care that she's dead. I'll cry for the people who are fucking worth it.

April—Isobel

Fuck. Not Isobel.

You never wanna think about your friends dying, but also, THAT'S ALL I DO ANYMORE. You have to, right, in this town, in this school. Especially if you're on the hero squad, and that's me and Dylan, Isobel and Isaac. Used to be Logan, too, but he died freshman year. Fucking zombies, man. That was a rough time.

It's stupid, I guess, but I always thought Isobel and Isaac would die on the same day. You know, they're not just Isobel and Isaac; they're Isobel-N-Isaac, a two-piece set, parts not sold separately. Some people even think they're twins, and they might as well be. Born two minutes apart in next-door delivery rooms, like, some real movie destiny shit. Isaac is the half-vampire, Isobel the wereboar. (Weregilt, I guess—cis girl, no teen pregnancy piglets, etc.— but she likes the sound of wereboar better, so.) Isobel and Isaac have a billion inside jokes, finish each other's sentences and everything. It's annoying as shit. They should have died *together*.

Instead, Isobel died alone on April Fool's, taking the

stake meant for Isaac's heart, and it's like. How do you even move on from that, right? Isaac's all fucked up now, obviously, and Dylan's trying to help—Dylan's the actual Hero of the hero squad, her whole job is checking in and giving pep talks and killing shit—but I'm just, IDK. I haven't cried in a long time.

I love Isobel. Not romantically—we dated for half a second back in seventh grade—but like. ~~We sing~~ We sang Blackpink together. We killed monsters together. She helped me research some old-as-shit magic shield spells, and I helped her study for physics tests. We played *what shape does this bloodstain look like* together. I should have cried for Isobel, right?

(Dylan's worried about me, too. She doesn't know about this notebook.)

May—Min-Seo

I've known Min-Seo since we were six, but also, we didn't know each other at all. Different churches, different neighborhoods—well, much as a town this small can *have* neighborhoods—different friends. I'm the loveable witchy weirdo on the hero squad. She's the lonely chess prodigy with bifocals and burn scars. We've never had much in common.

Still. For someone I talked to maybe twice a year, I liked Min-Seo well enough. She was pretty funny, actually, in this super dry, weirdly formal way, and absolutely did not give two shits about your wrong opinion—at least, not until The Day We Barely Averted the White Witch Apocalypse. (By we, I mean the hero squad. Min-Seo didn't avert shit. All she did was survive, which is more than I can say for the rest of the chess club, who mostly just exploded.) Min-Seo was...shakier...after that. And now she's dead because of a car accident, a fucking *car accident*, which is bullshit, it's not FAIR. Min-Seo should've at least lived long enough to see whatever the next Almost-End-of-Days would be. There's always some big doom bullshit around the last week of school. Last year it was the whole witch thing, the year before, the Near-Zombie Apocalypse. Saved the world, lost a Logan. Summer vacation always begins with blood.

And June, it's coming. It's only a few weeks away.

But Min-Seo, like. I always think of this group poetry project we had in 10th grade. It was me, Min-Seo, Olive (fucking Olive), and Dylan, and we each had to pick a poem and analyze, like, symbolism and shit. Olive picked "The Red Wheelbarrow" by William Carlos Williams because she's the actual worst person alive. Dylan wanted to pick "Brutal" by Olivia Rodrigo, but Mrs. Q has a bug up her ass about *song lyrics* being different than *poetry*; instead, Dylan Thom picked Dylan Thomas because she thought that was hysterical. Which nope, absolutely wasn't, but that's okay; it's MY job to be the comic relief. And yeah, the jokes have been morbid lately. Still, better me than Isaac, who usually gets distracted before he even makes it to the punchline, and better than Isobel, too, whose sense of humor boils down to puns and schadenfreude.

Anyway, *I* thought Dylan should pick "First Fig" by

Edna St. Vincent Millay because she's a 17-year-old basketball god AND unofficial Class Savior AND working unpaid shifts at her parents' burger joint, which means she knows all about burning the candle at both ends. ("*Actually*, Sparrow," Olive had said, "'First Fig' is about youth culture and partying too much. I thought everyone knew that." Shut the fuck up, Olive.)

I picked "Dirge Without Music," a different poem by St. Vincent Millay. Which, look, I know it's super weird to say you dream about a poem, but yeah, sometimes I do. It's like, I'm burying everyone, right, all the dead kids, all the dead teachers, all the dead moms and dead dads and dead cats and dead dogs, and there's this whisper—*down, down, down*—as roses grow from their graves. It's not my favorite dream, TBH, but it IS my favorite poem cause, like. It doesn't try to sugarcoat shit. It's not saying death is natural, appreciate the cycle, embrace the beauty of corpse-to-rose recycling. It's saying death sucks. It's saying I don't have to be at peace with shit.

Fuck. Talking about me again. Sorry, I'm sorry.

Anyway, Olive's going off on her "First Fig" and "anyone who's anyone" bullshit, and Min-Seo—so quietly confident before all her chess friends blew up—told Olive, "No one knows that because it's not true. 'First Fig' is almost excessively open to interpretation, which you'd know if you'd stop confusing your own anemic opinions for objective truth." Olive legit sputtered—it was beautiful —but Min-Seo ignored her, saying some critics thought "First Fig" might be about bisexuality, since ESVM was also bi (REPRESENT!) and then told us she'd picked a contemporary poem: "Vespers" by Louise Glück.

Olive hated it, obviously, because she only likes poets who are long dead, but *I* liked it. I mean. I didn't totally *get* it right away. You know, there were tomato plants? But I liked listening to Min-Seo recite it with this...slow, rising anger, this steely resolve. I liked how she spoke with her hands, even back then. How she said, "It's explaining fear and responsibility to God."

I wish we'd talked more last year. Maybe we had more in common than we thought.

June—Isobel-N-Isaac

Oh. Oh, I was right: they died on the same day, after all.

~~I don't. I can't.~~ Fuck. Okay, obviously, I lied earlier. Practicing my creative writing skills: the Agatha Christie, the unreliable narrator. I just don't know how to think about people anymore without eulogizing them, like, everyone's gonna die eventually, might as well get your mourning speech ready. It's not a new habit, really, imagining everyone I know dead, only ever since Liam got his throat ripped out, I've been writing my pretend-eulogies here—sometimes for the people who actually died (RIP, Mr. Moreno), and sometimes for people who just haven't died yet. Maybe I'm like, processing? Trying to prepare myself? But I think I'd wanted this journal to be a prayer, too, some kind of weird protection spell. Spells and prayers aren't so different really; magic just requires more ingredients, and you get more immediate results. Still, they're not always the results you want. And that's God, too: sometimes, the answer is no.

God said no a lot last week. Not to everything. We saved the world again. Two worlds, even. June 10th, The Day We Averted the Parallel Earth Apocalypse. And my bubble shield didn't fail, even though it was the biggest one I'd ever made, even though I almost died, holding it up so long. Knocked me out for two days, couldn't walk for the next four, but I saved the school and all the scared people hiding safely inside.

But that's the thing about being on the hero squad: you don't get to hide inside.

Isaac was born first and died first. We were idiots, we thought it was over, and Isaac was giving one of his super bouncy, high-on-adrenaline monologues, some prehistoric *Star Trek* mirror shit, IDK, he was THAT kind of nerd—and then The Breach opened up anyway, right where he was standing. He...halved, straight down the center. His mouth opened, and he fell apart. Dylan screamed. I screamed. Isobel just stood there, blank face, no one home.

And that's when the evil monologue began. Earth 2 Mr. Morales. I can pretty much guess what he would've said: you fell for my evil plot, these monsters were just a decoy, and now I will destroy both our worlds, no one should live if my wife/child/dog is dead. It's always some bullshit like that. But I guess we'll never know for sure cause that's when Isobel shifted, when she charged and broke all his bones with her big, boar-teeth. He got a few shots off first. Got her in the chest twice, which killed her, but E2 Mr. Morales died first, screaming. *Then* Isobel died, crawling back, reaching for what was left of Isaac.

But not much was left because that Breach just kept getting bigger, bigger, bigger.

(You know what else I was right about? I didn't cry for Isobel, not really. I was still crying for Isaac, see. Everything happened so fast. My brain couldn't catch up. I was still crying for Isaac when Dylan died.)

June—Dylan

I can't. I won't, I don't want to talk about that, I don't want to talk about the end. We all know what happened. We know what heroes always do when there are no other choices left.

You, whoever you are, whoever found this stupid Hello Kitty notebook, whoever's reading this stupid fucking diary and thinking, *whoa, this chick was fucked up*, you don't need to know the specifics, you don't need me to set the scene. Maybe you knew Dylan, maybe you were even there, hiding behind my old-as-shit magic shield and watching her stop the end of the world again. Maybe you saw the other Dylan, too, because she was there, of course she was. Every version of her is a hero, and every version of her is gone, and you might think you knew her, but you couldn't have, not like I did. Dylan wasn't your best friend. She didn't teach YOU how to defend yourself with a knife. She didn't paint YOUR toenails in bi pride or smuggle in food from her parents' restaurant when you didn't have anything to eat. Everyone knows Dylan's the only reason any of us made it to the junior year, but no one knows that her favorite M&Ms are yellow (they taste better, ~~she says~~ she said), and that worms totally freak her out (so that big demon-worm last Christmas was a real fucking problem), and that we met at church when we were eight (she stopped going after her dad died, and I let her rip up and draw all over my Bible, even though I still loved God back then). No one knows that she was scared a lot and angry a lot but always tried to hide it. No one knows how she got that "Vespers" poem right away, how she was just as haunted by responsibility, by tomato vines, as I am by roses. No one knows I was gonna bake a We Survived cake for graduation, and Isobel-N-Isaac were going to decorate it, and Dylan—okay, Dylan was just gonna eat, because she could hold her breath for 6 minutes and kill a demon in 4, but absolutely could not be trusted with frosting. No one knows any of that because everyone who did is dead, everyone but me.

Whoever reads this, whoever you are, you have to know how wonderful Dylan was. You have to know we didn't deserve her. You have to know how much we've lost.

June—Father Ryan

This fucking guy.

So, top secret: I used to have these weird daydreams about him. Nothing gross, you perv. He's like 40. It's just funny cause I'm not Catholic. Even my parents, who agree on *nothing*, agree that Catholicism is a drag. But Methodists don't have that whole 'sit in a weird box and spill your guts to some barely visible guy, who then says, "It's cool, my dude, God loves you, anyway."' I don't know, that used to seem really appealing to me. All cathartic and shit.

So yeah, I used to imagine these conversations. I'd end up at St. Eugene's somehow (my car stopped working, there was a storm, one of my friends was dead and I needed to scream about it—HA, only ONE of my friends was dead, what a fucking optimist I was back then), and I'd sit in that weird box and spill my guts, and Father Ryan would say something all enigmatic and profound, something that'd make me go, *Huh.*

I thought a lot about Father Ryan when I woke up from the coma, too, when I was too weak to stand and trying not to remember Isaac's body, Isobel's hands, Dylan's face. I wouldn't be confessing shit this time, though. This time, we'd talk poetry. I'd say, "Father, I get it now. Louise Glück was right. God is heartless." I'd say, "God never gives us more than we can handle, God gives us monsters so we can defeat them—but what if we CAN'T handle it, what if we CAN'T defeat them? Why do we have to follow God's plan when it's this fucking STUPID? Yeah, He has a plan, so what? Making a plan's not the same as *living* it. It's not God who does the work, who kneels in the dirt desperately trying to save His shitty tomatoes. It's not God who loses people, who's afraid every fucking second of his fucking life. God made the Garden, but we're the gardeners, and it's up to us. He's irresponsible as shit."

I imagined screaming all that, imagined Father Ryan's enigmatic compassion. Imagined feeling a tiny bit better instead of empty and furious and empty again. That's all I wanted from my weird little daydreams: some tiny spark of hope.

But then Father Ryan denied Isaac a Catholic funeral because vampires, even half-vampires, aren't welcome in the Kingdom of God. So, fuck that guy forever. I'm glad the carnivorous pixies got him. I hope their teeth were extra sharp. I hope they feasted slow.

July—Mom

Yeah, I'm a bad daughter, I get it, but honestly, this is Mom's own fault. Who lets her kid keep going back to school after THREE different near-apocalypses? Who doesn't move away after the very first zombie attack? But it's always *we can't afford to pick up and move* and *this is just life* and *there are zombies everywhere, Sparrow.* Which is true, it's all true, but also, Liam had to come from somewhere, right, somewhere without gullet-eaters? Some normal, faraway town with only 1/4 the monster population and a near-apocalypse every 5-10 years? I could be so happy in a town like that, maybe. Mom might still be alive there.

But fuck, don't listen to me. I'm an unreliable shit, remember? Even if there was some magical safe town, I never would've left the hero squad behind, not when they were alive. And now that they're dead, well. The fuck does it matter, right? My friends are gone, they're *rotting*; I'm not gonna be *happy*. I can't even act happy anymore. Who's got that kind of energy? Smiling, pretending to give a shit, eating every goddamn day. It's impossible. It's exhausting. Mostly, I just curl up in bed, staring at the walls and trying not to think too much. That's what I was doing when I found out about Mom. Lying on my bed, staring at nothing, maybe trying to BE nothing, and Dad knocks and knocks, but not like a monster's chasing him, so I take my time, cause fuck it. And Dad's crying even though he and Mom HATE each other, like hate-hate, like Shakespearian, and he says, "Sparrow, honey," and I'm all, "Oh, Mom's dead." Cause who else, right? Who else is left?

Fuck, I did it again. All me, me, me. I, I, I. I'm supposed to tell you about Mom, the good times, the bad, what her favorite flavor of M&M was, but I'm too tired to remember anything, and anyway, I really don't think she had one.

July—Dad

But what if it's Dad, right? What if *he* goes first? Yeah, that'd probably be easier, TBH. Wouldn't have to move. Wouldn't have to remind him I'm 17-years-old and I've helped stopped three different apocalypses, never mind all the monster of the week shit, so no, Dad, I actually don't want any Judy Moody books for my birthday, or unicorn stationary, or Hello Kitty *anything* because I am not a fucking CHILD. At least Mom talks to me like I'm an adult. At least she doesn't try to be my friend. Dad, you really wanna be friend, DO YOU KNOW WHAT HAPPENS TO MY FUCKING FRIENDS?

Yeah. Yeah, Dad died, he got eaten by a giant werebunny, sucks to be him. And you know what? My life barely even changed cause sure, I love the guy, I remember when he actually WAS there every day, when he made me animal-shaped pancakes and told me Bible stories in funny voices because he said God likes it when children laugh—but now I barely see him (work, always work, can you imagine what kind of apocalypse we'd face if a risk management analyst ever stopped analyzing risks), and he doesn't know me; he doesn't know me at all. I'll miss him, I'll dream about him lonely and dead in the ground, but my life won't be much different, and anyway, I know how to lose people and keep going. I'm fine.

August—Olive

I found her. I guess she didn't want to do it at home. Makes sense. Her mom, all those sisters. Lucy, Emma, Addy, Jo.

Olive wrote all their names down. She wrote *I'm sorry, I love you, I love you, I'm so sorry*.

It's good that I found her. Better, at least. They would've been so traumatized. They would've cried so much.

But she was supposed to go to Stanford. She was supposed to prove me wrong.

September—Sparrow

Well, obviously, I'm not dead yet. But I should probably write my own eulogy. Who knows? Maybe somebody will even still be alive to deliver it.

Here lies Sparrow Sykes, age 17. If only she'd made it two more weeks. 9 days shy of her 18th birthday, 13 days shy of senior year. We'll always remember how she dyed her hair bright colors and wore oversized flannel and dark leggings every day. She was a good student, well. A B's and C's student, anyway, but a good kid. Well. An okay kid. She did swear all the fucking time, and didn't love God like she used to, like she was supposed to, and also her handwriting was terrible, and she didn't have a thigh gap, and there was that one time with the premarital sex, the GAY premarital sex, even, and she was one fruit loop short of a dozen, and she sucked at both metaphors and math. But she was a good friend (except she outlived her friends) and a good witch (except for prediction spells, time travel spells, resurrection spells, fucking *useful* spells), and, well. She'd been young, anyway. What a pity. What a loss.

Maybe not so much of a loss.

My parents would be sad, at least. Dad would call me his little girl. Mom—I really don't know what Mom would say. She's not big on words, on letting people see stuff. Maybe my death would finally break her. Maybe she'd cry so hard she couldn't speak, or maybe she'd get up to the front of the church and say, *there are dead kids everywhere. That's just life.*

Olive knew that too, I think. Olive knew it was only a matter of time. "Because I could not stop for Death," and all that. Funny, none of us picking Emily Dickinson. Or Auden and that one sad poem from that old romcom about all the weddings. Dad loves that movie. I can't relate. I mean, it's just funeral after funeral after funeral here. That's what every tomorrow is, you know, someone else's funeral, if not your own. Mom's right: there's no escape from that. Zombies are everywhere. There's nowhere to run.

So, I can't stop thinking, did Olive have the right idea? Can't get out alive, so at least get out quick? It makes sense; it makes so much sense. It's the waiting that breaks you, isn't it? Not just the grief, but the inevitability. Not just the fear, but the despair. How long had Olive been planning it? Since the last near apocalypse? Before? She was at school that day. I know because I'm the one who pushed her inside. She was with all the other kids, watching through the windows, seeing Isobel-N-Isaac die, seeing Dylan die. Not that any of them were friends, but like. School's about to start, and our Class Savior is dead. And Olive, she was so smart. She was so obnoxiously smart, and she watched the hero squad bleed out, and I think she must've done the math. If there are 250 helpless high school students and an endless supply of monsters, what is the probability that 25 will die the first day back? If there are 30 coffins and six pallbearers, how many people will be successfully buried before the pallbearers all get eaten by werewolves? Maybe Olive just couldn't face the statistics anymore, not one more goddamn black dress. The unshakable, inescapable knowledge that we go the way of all flesh. Down, always down.

I hated Olive, I still hate her, but this—not for this. Every day, God goes about his business, He ignores us, He feeds us to the roses, and I just can't blame anyone for making an alternative timetable to His big, stupid plan. Or is that just my brain lying to me, saying Olive had the right idea, that I don't deserve to be here anyway if I can't do anything useful. *Oh, you saved everyone inside the school? Good job! But now they're hanging themselves one by one, so what did you even accomplish? Really, what good are you?* And yeah, I'm not that good. A good person wouldn't forget how to cry. A good daughter wouldn't imagine her own parents dead. A good sidekick wouldn't survive her hero, would never dare outlive her only friends.

When does a eulogy become a suicide note? How do you know when it's time to STOP?

Before, I used to imagine Dylan finding this journal. She'd have worried even more if she'd read all this shit. I've imagined other people finding it, too: Father Ryan, a few teachers, a cute new student who knew when it was safe to scream. But I don't think that's going to happen now. If someone stumbles across this journal, I think I'll be long dead. Maybe suicide, maybe a gullet-eater, maybe an apocalypse no one's around to avert.

It feels so fucking lonely. It must be so lonely to die.

Whoever you are, reading this…could you write one last entry, a better eulogy just for me? Say something kind about me. Lie, if you have to. I think that's probably the best ending any of us can hope to have. That there's someone still alive who loves you.

That you'll matter when you're gone.

September—Sparrow

Forgive me if this goes poorly. I've never written a eulogy before.

Perhaps that's unusual. Sparrow apparently wrote them for half the school, but by her own admission, she's patently unreliable. I've always preferred to be honest, which is why I'll tell you that Father Ryan—*not* eaten by carnivorous pixies, unfortunately, although we can always pray—doesn't allow eulogies at St. Eugene's, as they're generally discouraged by the Catholic Church. Matt was an atheist, though, and Rosa a Wiccan. I might've spoken at their funerals last summer, except I was still in the burn unit and, by then, had stopped speaking at all. That wasn't an intentional choice, exactly. My parents insist I'm being difficult. My cousins keep calling me stubborn, but it's more like…I was too heartsick to give anyone my words, and now they're all trapped in this ugly snarl inside my chest. I don't know how to untangle it. I don't remember how to let the words out.

I can write them down just fine, though. So, I should say, in case anyone else ever reads this, that—as of today—Sparrow Sykes is still alive.

She probably wouldn't want me to disclose that yet. *It breaks the dramatic tension*, she'd complain, as if that's something secret diaries are even supposed to have. But fake-out deaths are an asinine trope, and if you wanted this done differently, Sparrow, you should have given your Sanrio cry for help to someone else.

Presumably, it's obvious that I'm not dead, either, although reading about my own hypothetical death via traffic collision was certainly one way to start the morning. I'm not angry, though. Mostly. Everyone has their own coping strategies. Therapy is probably healthier than... whatever this is, but therapy runs its own risks, too. It's very difficult to spend months finding the right therapist, someone you trust, who you can actually communicate with, who doesn't deliver three folksy aphorisms per session or insist she "gets" Korean culture because she tried making dalgona once after watching *Squid Game*—only to lose that therapist three weeks later in a particularly vicious werewolf attack outside the only banh mi shop in a fifty-mile radius. Not to use an extremely specific example or anything.

At any rate, Sparrow and I once had precious little in common. I was the second gen Asian kid with a bowl cut and homemade lunches. She was the short, dimpled white kid with sloppy pigtails and thrift store clothes. I was the traumatized chess prodigy, both literally and figuratively scarred. She was the plucky sidekick, armed with Crayola hair and an iPhone grimoire. Sparrow had decent tastes in poetry, and I vaguely admired that she was brave, but I wasn't looking for her on that rooftop. I only wanted to catch my breath.

But Sparrow, I found you anyway, and you shoved this diary in my face.

A eulogy isn't quite a suicide note, and a suicide note isn't quite a poem, but perhaps they're all open to analysis, to varied interpretations. My interpretation is this: the speaker is grappling with grief, with loss of faith and existential despair. The speaker dreams of confession, of being found out, of being *seen*. Can near-strangers ever truly see one another? In this quasi-eulogy, I will posit that they can. We're both sole survivors, both high school seniors. We're lonely, haunted girls in a town forever on the verge of apocalypse. Maybe we're not friends. Maybe we stood on that school rooftop for different reasons—but still, we both stood there, looking down, down, down.

My interpretation is this: you don't want to end up like Olive. This is you trying to save yourself, to not go gentle. You know the rest.

It's last period now. You've been waiting all day to read this, still searching for that tiny spark of hope, the will to persevere. You want me to say something kind, correct? To say you'll matter when you're gone?

You will. But isn't it more important to know how you can matter while you're *here*?

So.

Sparrow and I met when we were children, but we didn't *know* each other until we were 18. Back then, we had to rely on one another a lot. We weren't very good at it, not right away. It's hard to learn how to hope again. It's hard to fight against your own brain. But Sparrow desperately need a reason to keep going, and I—I needed a friend, someone who understood what it meant to bear the weight of survival, someone who didn't mind communicating by text and DM and back-and-forth eulogy. And that was something we could do for each other; that was a way we could survive. Not forever, I know. We're all rose-food in the end, but we're also so much more before that. We're girls and women and poetry students and witches and chess prodigies and mourners and K-pop fans. We're more than tributes waiting to be written. We never surrendered. We never resigned.

Again, please forgive any inadequacies in this entry. Obviously, you're the eulogy expert here, but such expertise will take several attempts and hypothetical deaths to master. So, come back to school tomorrow, Sparrow. Read what I've written.

Give us more time.

September—Min-Seo

Also, Min-Seo obviously did *not* die in a car accident, as previously claimed. She died heroically, saving small children from a burning church fire, which inspired her new friend to stay in school and raise her English grades with a heartbreaking autobiographical essay about personal growth. Honestly, Sparrow. A car accident? Really?

October—Mr. Harrison

I didn't know him well. Seemed nice enough, but come ON. He was a substitute teacher. A very brave, very stupid substitute teacher who was immediately murdered by the ghost of a small, sacrificed goat. I feel bad for him, kind of, but also, I've got other shit going on.

First, Mom got a new boyfriend, and he non-ironically says things like "golly" AND drinks orange juice with pulp, so. He's either a Mormon or a secret demon that could potentially impregnate Mom with a stepbrother-Antichrist, gross. Then Dad caught me scribbling in this journal, which means he thinks I actually LIKE his awful presents, which means now I'm the lovable witchy weirdo with this horrifying Hello Kitty backpack. Also, Min-Seo has suddenly decided we should risk going to Homecoming, which is literally the worst idea anyone's ever had. A) Nobody asked me, and B) I thought I was trying to stay alive, remember? How many people died at the last dance, Min-Seo? Yeah, that's what I thought.

But—okay, if this is about wearing a hot ass dress and showing off your survivor scars, then fuck it, fine. But if we're doing this, we're bringing SO many weapons and incantations, and also, you're never allowed to reference

The Outsiders again. I'm giving you time to master your eulogy skills, I'm trying to have hope again, whatever. S.E. Hinton sucks, you don't get to die heroically or at all, and if you ever tell me to stay gold, I really will jump off this building and haunt your ass. And my English grades are fine, you bitch. It's MATH that's killing me.

And yeah, I know. Poor Mr. Harrison, did I forget about him? Well, kind of. Look, he's dead, so many people are dead, and I didn't magically learn to cry again, okay? If anyone ever reads this, thinking, *wow, Min-Seo can teach Sparrow how to weep, and Sparrow can teach Min-Seo how to talk*, like, stop being an asshole. Nothing comes that easy.

Min-Seo IS teaching me stuff, mostly chess strategies and how to French braid. In turn, I'm teaching her witchcraft. Not just her, either, but any student who wants to learn. Which not everyone does or, frankly, can. Also, this could backfire *very* badly. I am definitely keeping an eye out for any more prescriptive, white witch, mean girl bullshit. But we don't have Dylan or Isobel or Isaac anymore, so we've got to do something, right? Maybe we can all teach each other different ways to rescue ourselves, to keep from taking that last step off the ledge. Maybe instead of a hero squad we can have ~~an army~~, ~~a self-defense class,~~ a coven of survivors.

Look. I don't know what I'm doing. We're all going to die someday, and I'm still dreaming the same rose dreams, but I don't have to be at peace with that shit, right? I don't have to be grateful. My friends *mattered*. Min-Seo matters. *I* matter because I'm alive, because I want my survivor cake, because I'm funny, because I'm bi, because my favorite M&M's are blue.

God can have His roses. The tomato gardeners remain defiant.

IF WE
SURVIVE
THE
NIGHT

IF WE SURVIVE THE NIGHT

I T'S AUTUMN, AND all the dead girls are kneeling in the yard[1]. The sun is orange, low in the sky. It is Afternoon Contrition.

Heather doesn't know what year it is. She died in 1987: fucked out on a camp cot, sticky and unprepared. Not that anyone can prepare for a masked man and a screwdriver through the ear, but at least Mike didn't have his tits out. At least he got the chance to run.

Of course, Mike didn't make it, either. Harper confirmed it, but Heather already knew: she's been around long enough to know what kind of people survive the night. But Mike isn't at the house. None of the boys are. It's only the dead girls and the angel, walking between them, judging.

The angel is made from marble, and inexplicable, white feathers trail in his wake. He stands above her, perfect, glorious. "Heather. Will you repent?"

---

1. violence, murder, suicide, abusive language, psychological torture, gore.

Heather spits in his face. Or, she thinks about it. A year ago, she would have done—had done—without regret.

"Repent, Heather. If you are pure of heart, you will be forgiven."

Heather will never be forgiven. Rarely anyone is, no matter how sorry they are, how broken, how pure they try to be. The only girls who leave this house are not girls at all but puppets, limp, folded flaps of cloth that only expand into the shape the angel makes them.

Heather's afraid to be forgiven.

The new girl arrives at dinner. Megan barely glances up— another dead white girl, not exactly news, and she hates the introductory stories: I had sex, and I died. I did drugs, and I died. I'm Black, and I died.

There are twelve girls at the house—thirteen now—and eleven of them are white. "Pretty standard," Harper had said when she'd arrived, pale and shaking and bleeding from the back. "As victims, white people outnumber PoC, like, 10-1. Course, that's just cause the final girl is *always* white, so all her white parents, teachers, and buddies die too, along with her one Black friend, or the Asian stoner who brought the music."

Megan had been the one Black friend. Funny, to think that's all she boiled down to.

"They called yours the Waco Cheerleader Massacre," Harper had continued, though Megan hadn't asked. "Only three victims were cheerleaders, though, and that's including you."

"Jen?"

"Sure, she made it. Final girl. Brave little toaster."

That's good, at least. Mostly that's good.

"Looks like the Welcome Wagon's arrived," Heather says sourly, stabbing her lasagna. Megan glances up and sees Cindy greeting the new girl. She'd welcomed Megan, too, once upon a time, answered all her questions, showed her the bathrooms, the meal room, the open graves. And when Midnight Penance had come, Cindy ran without looking back.

Megan doesn't blame her. It's the instinct. It still takes over, even after all this time.

Glass breaks, and Megan's breath catches—but it's only Harper, staring at the new girl. Milk and broken shards all around her feet.

The new girl steps forward. "Harper?"

"But." Harper pushes up her glasses, like that might make someone else appear. "You should have survived. I did the research. Why didn't you survive?"

The new girl has red hair, and a hole in the back of her head. Impaled, probably.

"I did survive," the new girl says, crying. "I survived, and I *died anyway*."

Harper makes Abby a cup of tea. It's a soothing liquid, the universal sign for *calm the hell down*, and Abby thinks it'd be a lot more successful if the girl who made it hadn't taken a fire axe to the back exactly one year ago.

It had been Abby's ex-boyfriend who'd killed Harper. He'd killed eleven people, actually, but not Abby—Abby had shot Ethan three times in the chest and then once in the head, just to make sure. They had to give Abby a lot of tea that night. But she came through it, she survived, she went to therapy six times a week and moved away to college so she could start fresh—

—Only to find someone wearing Ethan's reptilian mask in her dorm. She opened her mouth to scream. He shoved a piece of rebar through it.

Abby sits on a sofa, sips her tea, and waits for it to make sense.

The tan girl with the Farrah hair—Cindy, Abby thinks, or Cathy—is sitting near her feet, peering up, uncomfortably close. Her eyes are fine china blue and blink inconsistently, like a broken doll. "Did you start doing drugs? Or have sex?"

"I told you," Harper says impatiently. "Sex doesn't matter anymore. The first documented non-virgin to survive a killing spree was back in 1981, and final girls have regularly survived losing their virginity since 1996."

"1995," a cheerleader says. There are three different cheerleaders here. This one is tall and Black and wearing a red crop top uniform. Abby notices a frayed yellow cord around the girl's wrist. There's blood spattered all over it.

"Really?" Harper asks, surprised. "I thought—"

"You must have done something wrong," Cindy/Cathy says. "You wouldn't be here if you hadn't."

"I didn't do anything," Abby snaps, even though she's not always sure that's true. She knows what people said, after Ethan. She knows how they looked at her. "Anyway, I don't even know where here *is*."

She turns to Harper, the only familiar face. They'd never been friends, but they'd held hands under the bleachers, shaking as Ethan killed the Homecoming Queen. "You said, you said this was Purgatory, but I—"

A girl laughs. She has blonde crimped hair and heavy eyeliner and a bloody ear she keeps tugging on. "This is Hell," the girl says. "Don't let anyone tell you differently."

"It's Purgatory," Cindy/Cathy hisses. "If we repent, if we're forgiven—"

The lights flicker, and suddenly several girls are on their feet. "What is it?" Abby asks. "What's happening?"

Cindy/Cathy smiles with her wet, broken doll eyes.

"Penance," she says.

Heather is the first to die that night. A girl falls, running through the woods, and Heather stops to help her. She takes a knife to the spine for it.

Harper waits until another girl screams in the distance, then climbs down the tree and steps around Heather's body. Staying in the tree indefinitely never works; she's tried it before. She's tried everything before. Nothing works.

She goes back to the house and finds Abby in the kitchen, clinging to the telephone. Her eyes are showing too much white. "Somebody answered it. Somebody—but the line—"

"Yeah, it does that," Harper says. The phone is a sick joke, one that new girls always fall for. Harper had, anyway, dialing 911 with bloody fingertips, like there was a police unit waiting for the call. *Roger that, on route to the afterlife.*

She assumes it's the angel on the other end, phone in one hand, knife in the other—although the killers, while varying in height, weight, mask, and preferred weapon, all rather noticeably lack wings. Maybe angels shapeshift with the moon, like lycanthropes. The moon is always full here.

"But why—"

"It's a contest," Harper explains. She rummages through the drawers until she finds a steak knife, like that will help. "You have to survive until dawn. If you're the final girl, you get to leave."

"If not?"

Cindy staggers into the kitchen, covered in too much blood. She's dead, even if she doesn't know it yet. Abby screams when Cindy hits the floor.

"Don't worry," Harper says. "She'll be fine in the morning. We all will."

"Wait," Abby says, as Harper turns to leave. "Can't we, can't you—please, Harper. Help me."

Harper closes her eyes. Opens them. Looks at the girl she daydreamed about in math class, the girl she once gave a Star Wars valentine to, the girl who couldn't love her back.

"How'd that turn out for me last time?" Harper asks, and when Abby can't answer, leaves her behind.

There is nothing. There is darkness. Not even darkness. Void.

And then—

Cindy gasps, searching for air and only finding a mouthful of dirt to swallow. Loose, moist soil—she's covered in it, coated in it. She's breathing in her grave.

She fights back, struggling up, frantically pushing towards the surface—and cold, stone fingers take her by the hand, lift her up and out of the ground. There are no wounds to her stomach, only old ones to her chest that will never heal.

"Rejoice, Cynthia," the angel says. "You have been chosen for Resurrection. Another chance you'll have to join God in his Kingdom."

Cindy has lost count of how many chances she's been given, over the past forty years.

"Thank you," Cindy says, weeping. "Thank you, thank you, thank you…"

Breakfast is oatmeal, fresh fruit, and yogurt. Megan gets an extra piece of pineapple for being the last girl to die.

"I don't like pineapple anyway," Heather says, dumping the fruit on Megan's plate. Megan doesn't call her on the lie. Heather will turn anything into an argument these days.

"Anyway," Heather continues. "At least I wasn't standing in front of a window, *like an amateur*." She glares

133

at Abby. "How did you even survive your actual massacre?"

Abby flinches. "This happens every night?"

"Yup. It's Resurrection, then oatmeal. Tuna sandwiches, then Contrition. Lasagna, then Penance. The angel runs a tight, blood-spattered ship. I swear, if I could just order some *fucking pizza*, it wouldn't—oh. Oh, tell me you went for the phone. You did, didn't you? That's so precious—"

"Lay off," Harper says. "Everyone goes for the phone or the car the first night."

Megan had run for the car and ended up with a slit throat. Again. She eats her second piece of pineapple. It tastes like the oatmeal, which tastes like the tuna, which tastes like graveyard dirt when you close your eyes.

"Besides," Harper says, "you wanna talk amateur moves? How about helping up Cindy?"

Megan blinks. Heather doesn't even like Beth. Not that Heather likes anyone. Still—

"Sure, I helped her," Heather says, shrugging. "That's what heroines do, right?" She grins, no teeth. "Only the virtuous survive, isn't that the lesson? Only the brave? How about it, Abby? Didn't you at least try to help Harper back in the day?"

Abby pushes away from the table violently. Her bowl of oatmeal nearly upturns. Harper watches, something like regret in her eyes...but she doesn't chase after her.

Megan knows something about what real survivor girls do. She doesn't say anything.

Heather laughs and grabs Abby's pineapple. "Christ,

she's easy," Heather says. "Hey, does the pineapple taste especially good to anyone else today?"

Abby cries through Contrition. Harper tries not to look at her, instead staring straight through the angel as he cradles her face with his cold, stone hand. "Are you ready to live in the Kingdom of God, Harper? Are you ready to be forgiven?"

She is. She's exhausted of dying, of the constant, unshakable fear. She's already confessed so many petty sins, what's that word Catholics use—venial. Stealing candy. Selling papers. Sneaking out to the library, researching anything Google couldn't tell her, about serial killers, survivor girls, dead girls, her mother. Dad didn't talk about her mother. He wouldn't tell Harper how many times she'd been stabbed.

The Chronicle had told her, though: 27. Was Mom somewhere in a house like this? Had she repented? Had she been forgiven?

Harper wants to be forgiven, and yet...

Her eyes slide to Abby, helplessly; Abby, who'd been a B student with a great laugh, who'd once literally helped a little old lady cross a street. Abby, whose mother had never been tragically murdered, who sometimes smelled liked pot and cheated on her vegetarianism whenever chicken nuggets came around.

Abby, who Harper had shoved out of the way and taken an axe to the back for her trouble.

Abby had always been the frontrunner, the only possible Final Girl. It didn't matter that Harper had been an A student who didn't drink, didn't do drugs, who cried anytime she saw an animal cruelty commercial. It didn't matter because statistics didn't lie, and survivor girls, they were always straight.

"No," Harper says, because that's not something she wants to ask forgiveness for, not yet.

That night, Cindy doesn't run.

There's a warning behind her, palms frantically slapping against the window. She ignores it. "You're doing God's work," Cindy tells the killer. "I'll wait for your judgment."

The killer is tall, taller than he was last night. He walks slowly, like the masked men of her time, not like the ones who take limbs first and lives later. This killer will draw nothing out. He has a job to do, and Cindy, she is the job.

Still, when he steps toward her, knife raised, her lungs—they stop working altogether because they *know*, because they remember, and they want no part of this self-sacrifice. Her lungs are not courageous. They do not care if she makes it to the Kingdom of Heaven. They only want to keep breathing; they only want to survive.

The killer knows about her lungs, of course; he knows about all the traitorous bits inside of her: her heart, beating too fast, her stomach, cramped up tight. It's no surprise when he judges her unworthy, when the knife plunges into her chest.

She will begin again tomorrow. The angel, he will give her another chance. Cindy will be forgiven someday, she knows.

But that's not what her lungs know, as she chokes on blood.

"She's such—who's that fucking *dumb*? It doesn't work, nothing works, and she's just—she—"

"Heather," Megan interrupts, stepping around Cindy's body. "Why do you even care?"

Heather doesn't care. Or she shouldn't. She closes Cindy's blue eyes for absolutely no reason at all, then slaps her across the face and tells her that she's a poofy-haired Jesus fucker who's too dumb to live. Heather may be crying. She does that sometimes. It doesn't mean anything.

Megan is holding two pokers. She offers one to Heather, warily. Megan has always been wary, even by dead girl standards. Some of the girls are friends and some are enemies, but Megan has always held herself apart, just on the outside, watching. Megan very rarely cries.

Heather looks down at Cindy. "She used to be different, you know. When I got here, she was a whole other person. Not..."

"A poofy-haired Jesus fucker?"

"...Broken."

Megan raises an eyebrow at Heather's tear-stained face and bloody knees. "I think we're all pretty broken."

But they're not, not like Cindy. Not like the cloth girls,

the forgiven. Lisa survived the night not long after Heather first arrived, and Mary and Chris were already half out of their minds, but Cindy...

"She was my friend," Heather says quietly, and then the killer appears.

He doesn't walk through the doorway. He just appears, and Heather barely pulls Megan back in time. "Get out of here!" she yells, pushing Megan behind her.

"You—"

"Go!" Heather says, and Megan goes, scrambling out the window while Heather swings the poker at the killer's head. He staggers, but gets back up. Killers always get back up. It's not a fight she can win.

That's not why she fights.

She swings and swings, her fifth crack knocking the mask to the floor. She falters, and that's all it takes: his knife is now inside her.

"Mike," Heather whispers.

Mike pulls out the knife, cradles her. Stabs the blade through her ear.

It takes Abby a long time, remembering how to breathe. The other girls catch their breath with ease while she shudders by her grave, coughing up mouthful after mouthful of dirt. Abby still needs practice at Resurrection.

By the time she heads inside, everyone's already at breakfast. Some have showered, but most are just eating their oatmeal and strawberries with their grave dust still clinging to them. Harper, she sees, has two strawberries.

This is what Abby will be doing for—for forever. She will eat strawberries and confess and die. She will crawl out of the ground and be put back into it. She will crawl out of the ground—she will crawl out of the ground—

"Hey." Harper takes her by the arm, leads her to one of the tables. "It's okay. Just breathe through it."

It's not okay; it's not. This is *forever*—

"Just breathe, Abby."

It's a long time before she can.

Someone's grabbed her a breakfast tray. Abby drags her spoon through the oatmeal. If she vomits, Heather will be merciless. She knows what mean girls are like.

But Heather is staring blankly at her breakfast. Beside her, Megan frowns. "Hey," she says. "What's with you?"

Heather doesn't move.

Cindy leans across the table. "Heather? Have you finally seen the light?"

Heather laughs. She's also crying, which Abby finds unnerving. "I saw him. I saw his face."

"The killer?" Harper asks. "Was it the angel?"

Heather shakes her head. "I don't understand. I don't understand. It can't, it *wasn't*, but now—"

Megan takes Heather's hand. "Hey. Look at me."

Heather looks at her.

"You knew him? You knew the killer?"

Heather blinks. "It was Mike. My boyfriend, or. We weren't serious, but we were screwing around when the killer…the camp. 1987. He killed me. He killed me? Mike didn't kill me, but *he killed me*."

Everyone stares at her. Then they turn to Harper.

"Mike Kaminsky died in 1987," Harper says. She doesn't even have to think about it. "The Camp Chastain killer was a disfigured lunatic who escaped from a mental asylum and murdered eight people, including Heather *and* Mike."

"Lunatic?" Abby asks. "Isn't that kind of—"

"The 80's were big on mommy issues, deformities, and revenge," Harper says. "A compassionate understanding of mental illness, not so much."

"So maybe this guy didn't do it," Megan says. "Maybe the research is wrong."

"Hey. Do I tell you how to spell things or kick really high? My research is solid."

Megan shrugs. "It's been wrong before."

Harper resists the urge to throw her oatmeal at Megan's indifferent face. It's not like she's just casually insulting Harper's *life's work* or anything. "Okay, maybe I missed that your BFF was some secret slut—"

"Harper," Cindy chides, presumably because only the angel gets to call anyone a slut.

"—but missing a frame-up job? That's something else. Trust me: this guy was guilty as hell."

"Well, maybe Mike was in on it," Abby suggests. "Maybe they were partners?"

And Harper likes Abby, she really does, but who even

thinks like that? How would a stoner jock with no tragic backstory or otherwise notable family history somehow team up with a random mental patient who only happened to escape that night because of a freak electrical storm, anyway?

"Serial killers didn't start teaming up until the 90's," Harper says, instead of calling her childhood crush an idiot. "And Mike wasn't evil. He just…died."

"Well, he seems pretty fucking evil now," Heather says. Mascara drips down her face, and it looks like war paint. "If he wasn't the killer then, why is he the killer *now*?"

"Maybe he wasn't," Megan says.

"Fuck you. I know what I saw. I'm not crazy."

"I'm sure that's not what Megan meant," Harper says, even though that's obviously what Megan meant. "He did *act* like an 80's slasher. Maybe it's generational, a learned behavior. Kill as you saw others killed. Kill as you yourself were killed. And it's obviously not Mike every night, so maybe…well, we've all wondered, haven't we? Where the dead boys go?"

"You think they become killers?" Abby asked. *"Why?"*

"Well," Heather says, pushing up from the table, hands shaking but jaw set. "There's someone we can ask about that."

Heather attacks the angel like she does pretty much everything: whole-heartedly, and without much forethought. In all the years Megan's been here, she's never seen anyone try to hurt him before. Try to run, yes. Attempt suicide, yes. But no one has ever punched the angel, has thrown their entire body into it, screaming with thirty years' worth of accumulated fury and grief. There's something almost…religious…about the experience.

Of course, the angel is still made from marble, so he barely sways back, while Heather breaks her hand.

Cindy pulls her away. Heather's bent over, cradling broken, bleeding fingers. Red drips over the autumn leaves. "Who are the killers?"

"They are servants of God, as are we—"

"Bullshit. Was it Mike, last night?"

"Their mortal lives are unimpor—"

"Was it Mike?"

The angel looks at her calmly. "Yes."

"He—what about Steve? Rick—"

"Will a list help you achieve redemption?" The angel begins reciting names, although Megan doesn't recognize any at first, not until Jesse.

Jesse.

The first time he'd kissed her, it had been under the full moon. She wonders how he'd killed her, when he'd killed her. How many times he had killed her.

"So, it's true," Megan says. Her voice sounds distant to her own ears. "The boys are always killers, and the girls are always killed."

"Different punishments must be given," the angel says. "Different lessons must be learned."

Heather laughs. "Yeah? What's Mike's lesson? How to

kill efficiently? Creatively?" She tugs her ear. "Nostalgically?"

"Mike's penance is not your penance," the angel says, and turns back to the open graves. "You will learn nothing from this, any of you. We will speak of your sins at Contrition."

He moves towards the shovel, and Heather breaks free, grabbing it first and throwing it behind her. "I think we should talk about sin now."

The angel tilts his head. "Do you wish to confess?"

"No, I know why I'm here, and fuck you, fuck you if you think you can make me sorry." Heather spits in his face, and then blinks. Grins viciously and does it again.

The angel ignores the saliva dripping down his stone cheek. "If you do not wish to—"

"I want you to tell me why *they're* here." Heather looks around wildly, points at Abby. "That bitch, start with her. She was good enough to survive Round 1. Why not Round 2? What sin did she commit to condemn her to *this*?"

Abby shrinks back. She looks at Harper, then away.

"You left her," Megan says. She's surprised it took her so long to realize it. "You left Harper behind, didn't you?"

"No," Harper says, stepping forward. "No, I pushed her out of the way. I did that. That's not on her."

Abby doesn't look up. "You died because—"

"No," Harper says again. "Look, the other night, I didn't mean it, okay? I don't regret it, saving you. I loved you. Since, like, second grade and macaroni necklaces, I loved you, or, or something like love, anyway. You know that, right? You know how I felt?"

Abby nods. "I know, I knew. But I'm not, I'm sorry—"

"I know," Harper says. "That's okay. You don't owe me for that."

Abby finally meets her eyes. "You died for me."

Harper shrugs. "If it makes you feel better, I was always going to die."

"Oh, I didn't—you were sick?"

Harper closes her eyes, probably so she doesn't roll them. "I'm talking statistics, Abby, not disease. Research doesn't lie. Geeks are more mainstream these days, and a dead mom, well, that gets you a little leeway to be weird. But a lesbian, you know. That's just not survivor girl material."

"Harper—"

Harper keeps trying to smile. "I always knew. I tried not to be one, for a while, and then I thought maybe I could live some other kind of story. But stats don't lie."

"They lie," Megan says. "Harper, they lie all the time."

Harper looks at her, tired. "You keep insulting my research."

"Not your research," Megan says. "The facts."

"Facts are facts."

"Not if you know how to spin them. Not if there aren't any witnesses left behind."

"What—"

"She left me," Megan says. "Jen left me behind."

They'd been friends since fifth grade. No one was the bad girl. No one was the good girl. Megan was a cheerleader, a reader. She'd lost her virginity at fifteen. She sang, mostly at church. Jen didn't go to church. She wasn't a morning person. She ran canned food drives at the school, and had sex with her boyfriend in the boy's locker room. Jen gave Megan a friendship bracelet when they were twelve, and Megan wore it every day.

Megan fell by the pool, while the killer was chasing them, and Jen looked back, and there was time, there was time.

But the instinct took over. Jen ran, and Megan died.

"I don't blame her," Megan says, even though she had, bitterly, for the first few years. "But they said she was a hero, right? Brave, you said. I think that's just what everyone needed her to be. And the dead—you know who Brad Marsh was?"

"Jen's classmate," Harper says.

"Mr. Gunn?"

"Her cheerleading coach."

"What about me?"

"You're Megan King."

"But who *was* I?"

Harper inhales. "Jen Markham's best friend."

Megan smiles. Fingers the bloody, yellow bracelet around her wrist. "And all this time," she says, "I thought she was *my* best friend."

For a long moment, there's silence, only the rustling of dead leaves and white feathers in the wind. Cindy looks to the angel for guidance, but he only watches them impassively, unfeeling. Unconcerned.

No, she reminds herself. No, he only wants us to discover our own answers, our own Redemption. He watches us with love.

Because he has to love them, he has to, or else—

Heather turns on Abby. "Is that what they said about you, princess? That you were somehow better?"

Abby begins to cry, and Harper steps in front of her, a knight clad in a plaid shirt and tight, ripped jeans. "Jesus, would you stop being a bitch for two seconds and listen?"

Heather grins. Cindy knows that grin. She steps between them, squeezing Heather's shoulder gently.

"Enough," she says. "Who are you trying to hurt?"

Heather's mouth opens, but she doesn't answer, which is answer enough. Heather has never known herself.

"You must be calm," Cindy says. "This is not the way we find Redemption."

Abruptly, Heather pushes Cindy off. "We? We? The fuck you even need redemption for, Cindy?"

Cindy looks down. "You've heard my Contrition many times."

Heather snorts. "Yeah, yeah. Big Bad Cindy has sex on the couch while the kids are asleep. So the fuck what?"

"It was wrong," Cindy hisses.

"Yeah," Heather agrees. "You're a lousy fucking babysitter. You definitely deserved to get fired. Getting murdered, though? Getting murdered for forty fucking years?"

"Seems like overkill," Harper says, and a few other girls nod.

It's—no. No, they're wrong, of course they're wrong. If

she didn't deserve to be here, then she wouldn't be here. Maybe she'd thought differently once, that she'd been punished enough for such a simple sin—but that was just the Devil in her mind again, traitorous as her lungs. She belongs here. She has to.

"I was irresponsible," Cindy says. "Wicked. I was—"

"Sixteen," Megan says.

"No," Cindy says, even though that's true. "I'm—I'm—"

"Bad?" Heather asks. "Please. You don't know the first thing about being a bad girl."

"You do," Megan says, and Heather laughs.

"Oh yeah. Drinking, drugs...I was a total mega slut, sucked and fucked my way through the football team, the hockey team, hell, the debate team. I'm not sorry for any of it." She turns to the angel. "You hear me? I'm not sorry for shit!"

"You need redemption, Heather," the angel says.

"Bullshit."

But it's Megan, not Heather, who says it.

Heather laughs uneasily. "Look, I appreciate this whole dead sisterhood solidarity, or whatever, but I'm not like you guys, okay? I get why I'm here."

"You're here to be forgiven," Cindy says. "We're all—"

"You don't need forgiveness, you fucking cow, don't you get that yet?"

"You don't get it," Harper says, sounding stunned. "Both of you. All of us."

"The fuck are you—"

"Why did you save my life last night?" Megan asks.

Heather blinks. "Because—because to survive the—"

"No," Megan says. "You don't want forgiveness, remember? You have nothing to prove, so why the sacrifice? Why the bravery?"

"What's to fear?" Heather's grin keeps slipping at the edges. "It's not bravery if you're guaranteed resurrection."

But she's wrong about that, Cindy knows. The fear stays in your bones. Your body knows to be afraid. Your body remembers everything.

"You saved someone else, right?" Abby asks, and Cindy nods. In fact, all the girls do. "Sounds like the kind of thing a final girl does."

"Or is supposed to," Megan says.

"I didn't save anyone," Heather reminds them.

Cindy looks at Heather's ruined ear and realizes, "You didn't get the chance."

But if Heather hadn't died so quickly, wouldn't she have tried? Cindy thinks maybe she would have—and that means something, that's important, surely that's more important to God than sex or drugs or whatever else Heather had done wrong. What if Cindy has been wrong all these years? What if she's been the weak one, the wicked one, all along?

She doesn't know. She doesn't know. She looks to the angel, but he's still just standing there, removed, unmoved.

"I'm not a good girl," Heather says, shaking. "I'm not."

"What's a good girl?" Abby asks, and for the first time in years, Cindy isn't sure.

"If you're trying to make a point," Heather says, "why don't you just fucking make it?"

Abby isn't trying to make a point. She honestly doesn't know. The qualifications keep shifting. At first, she'd been a good girl: that poor thing, that brave thing, what a dreadful tragedy to befall her, and then—

"Why did you love me?" she asks Harper.

"Because...I don't know." Harper shrugs. "You helped me with that necklace, and you have red hair and freckles, and you thought Hufflepuff was superior to Gryffindor, even though Ravenclaw clearly trumps all, and you, you're you. I don't know, I don't really understand what you're asking."

"You died because you loved me."

"Look, we already—"

"You didn't kill anyone because you loved me," Abby says.

What a tragedy, they said, but what *causes* something like that, what so drastically changes a good, young man—someone with a top GPA, someone going places—into a killer? Why was he so obsessed with his ex-girlfriend? How did he fall so desperately in love? She was pretty, but she wasn't *beautiful*. She was nice, but she wasn't a *saint*. All those people he killed for her. What did she do to him? What did she *do*?

"Is that my contrition?" Abby asks the angel. "Am I being punished for Ethan's sins?"

"Ethan's penance is not your penance."

"But that's why I'm here, right?" There's something inside Abby now, something shaking, impatiently waiting to explode. "Because I led him down the dark path, because I tempted him to sin, because he killed all those people for me?"

"That's stupid," Harper says, even as the angel says, "Yes."

Different lessons must be learned, the angel had said.

Harper can't stop thinking it; everything else around her is a sort of buzz, a white noise that she can feel just underneath her skin. *Different lessons must be learned*, and Harper, she must be a pretty slow learner after all, because only now does she finally, finally understand what the angel has been trying to teach her all along: that being selfless is meaningless if you're a slut, that it's more important to be white than to be brave, that a girl will be punished and repent for a boy's sins, that the boy is never to blame. And this whole thing, this WHOLE THING—

"It's fucking Adam and Eve," Harper breathes, and then she's crying, and Cindy's on her knees, and Megan's making the first real facial expression Harper's ever seen her make. And then Abby's screaming, something wordless and *furious*.

Abby is launching herself at the angel, swinging the shovel at his head.

White slivers of stone fly through the air, barely more than a small handful of dust...but that dust is wet, and coated with blood. The angel lifts his hand to the thin crack in his cheek, and his lips part as his fingertips come away red.

"But..." the angel says, and winces.

Heather inhales, or gasps, or chokes.

It *hurts*; it feels like her lungs are collapsing, it feels like —no, that's not what it feels like at all. It feels like her lungs are *expanding*, that they've been shuttered for years, and she's only just remembered how to breathe.

The angel can bleed, so long as you hit hard enough. He can feel. He can feel *pain*.

And he didn't know—

—But Heather does.

Now she does, and now they do too. She can see it on the dead girls' faces. They know what it means, to feel pain. They know what they have the power to *do*.

No one is kneeling in the yard anymore.

"You can't," the angel says, but Heather can, so she takes the shovel and slams it straight into his face.

Blood bursts from his nose. He staggers back and makes a sound from the back of his throat like glass shattering into pieces. "You can't," he says again. "Another will come. This isn't the way to Redemption—"

But then they're on him, the shovel passing from girl to girl, slamming it into his throat and chest and kneecaps, everywhere blood and chunks of stone. They're speaking, sometimes screaming, out of breath and overlapping one another, their voices individual and somehow one.

"We are not your fucking cloth girls."

Heather slams the shovel down, shattering the angel's wings.

"Our penance is now your penance. But we're teaching you something new."

Harper shoves the angel, off-balance, into one of the open graves.

"We reject your Kingdom of God, your Redemption. We will *not* repent."

Cindy shovels dirt and listens, unmoved, to the angel's glass screams.

"We're done paying for someone else's sins. It's your turn to seek salvation."

Abby stays the shovel and forces the angel to climb out of the grave on crumbling hands and knees.

"When the dead boys come, when your friends come, when *God* comes, don't fight the instinct."

Megan pushes the angel forward through the autumn leaves and raises the shovel over her head.

"Now, angel. Now, it's your turn. Go. *Run*."

EVERY DAY IS THE FULL MOON

EVERY DAY IS THE FULL MOON

T HERE ARE THINGS you know and things you don't know[1]. You find it helpful to make lists. For example:

THINGS YOU KNOW:

- *A Wrinkle in Time* is bullshit. You don't care if it's Riley Chu's favorite childhood book, because she also identifies with Holden Caulfield, and thinks spiders are adorable. Riley's opinions are not to be trusted.
- Cafeteria food is the worst. The hamburgers taste like dog meat. You're better off bringing food from home, or developing anorexia.
- You tried becoming anorexic once because you wanted more visibly unhealthy coping mechanisms. It didn't take.

---

1. violence, mention of eating disorders, emotional and psychological abuse, abusive parent, domestic abuse/violence, blood/gore, possession.

- Your father is a werewolf, but mostly he's just an asshole.

"It's the night before the full moon," your mother says. "You know how he gets."

Your mother is a Valkyrie. Her wings are glorious, golden and impossibly large. She flies into battle, wars all over the world, and carries the valorous dead to their own particular Valhallas, bringing the same passion to the battlefield that she brings to everything in her life: teaching you to cook, watching UFC, vanquishing garden gnomes.

You want to be just like your mother when you grow up. And you don't want to be anything like her at all.

"Just a few more days," she says, as your father, howling, throws an entire bookcase across the room. "Just try not to upset him, okay? It'll all be over soon."

THINGS YOU KNOW:

- It will not all be over soon.

School, the next day. Riley has bravely sought out lunch in the cafeteria; you and Lea, less foolish, are hanging out in the quad. Lea is short and Black and gay and pretty, basically the polar opposite of you, and sometimes, when you're feeling petty, you tell yourself that at least you have bigger boobs and a better vocabulary. Unfortunately, she's winning in math, science, PE, dating, functional family dynamics, and general popularity, not that it's a competition or anything. Also, she's a faerie, which you both figured out last summer when you woke up with her newly grown green wings digging into your back.

You hate that you're jealous of your best friend, that you've always been jealous, even before she became something. Sometimes, it seems like you're the only senior left who hasn't become anything, and maybe aren't going to.

"Come over after school?" Lea asks, stealing a handful of your chocolate muffin. "You can explain that sonnet to me, and we can all get ready for the dance."

"Yeah. About that—"

"Nope," Lea says. "You're not doing this to me again, B. We bought dresses. We bought tickets. We're going to the dance."

"I'm just not—"

"You'll feel it," Lea says, a little grimly. "When you're *at the dance*."

Apparently, you're going to the dance.

At least, Lea doesn't ask to get ready at your house. She knows you why you never want to invite anyone home.

THINGS YOU DON'T KNOW:

- Why Lea wants you at the dance at all, since she'll probably just make out with Riley the whole time.
- How to walk in high heels without falling on your face.
- What you want to become, when you finally, hopefully, become something. Not a werewolf, obviously, and not a faerie, either—you'd only be the mammoth faerie standing by Lea's side. You've always wanted to travel, though, or at least, you wanted to leave. Maybe you could become something with wings to carry you far from home, although Mom's wings always carry her back there, in the end. You do love to walk. Sometimes you daydream about walking out for good, taking to the open road and following it until it ends in ocean…and then, maybe, just walking a little further.
- If having suicide fantasies means you ought to talk to someone, or just that you're a teenager, and you've probably watched *Point Break* too many times.

Despite yourself, you're having fun at the dance, especially since you tossed your size 12s into the community shoe pile. It's comforting that even girls with tinkling laughs and delicate bone structures can't dance in those things forever.

Riley has a delicate bone structure but doesn't exactly

tinkle. She's wearing combat boots with a black tulle dress and eyeliner as thick as your wrist, and she's not exactly gentle when she forcibly pulls you away from your very comfortable, very non-judgmental wall. "I had a vision of you dancing with me," Riley says matter-of-factly, like that isn't the biggest line of bullshit you've ever heard, like oracles can just go around predicting their own future. "Can't fight fate, right?"

"Guess not," you say dryly, although secretly you wonder. You find fate a depressing concept, the very opposite of freedom. What if it leads you nowhere at all? What if there really is no escape?

Your maudlin must be showing, because Riley's expression softens, her default "fight me" eyebrow slowly sinking away. "Come on, bitch," she says gently. "Dance with me, okay?"

You do. It's silly and a little awkward—you both keep trying to lead—but it also makes you laugh, especially when she tries to dip you and you both end up nearly falling to the floor. "We are not the most graceful people," you say, giggling, as you eventually right yourself.

"I don't know what you're talking about," Riley says. "I'm graceful like a motherfucker."

"Are motherfuckers especially graceful?"

"Yes," Riley says, just to be contrary.

Lea comes back from the bathroom just as Riley goes to grab a soda, threatening a three-way slow dance upon her return that will clearly only end in disaster. Only she doesn't return, so Lea goes after her while you head back to your wall. When Lea doesn't come back either, you're pretty sure they ended up in the backseat of her car. You never got the appeal of car sex. Maybe if you were a short shit like Lea, but you tower over the boys in your class, and not in a gorgeous model way, but like an extra in a Thor movie. It's one of the reasons you hate dances: it's impossible to find anything in your size. "Why don't you wear a suit?" a perky store clerk once asked. "Schools are much more progressive these days. Everyone likes *Modern Family*, right?"

You never know what to say, when people assume you're a lesbian or trans. Riley always knows; she just can't turn her mouth off, which means she ends up threatening to cut a bitch, a habit that's gotten her into plenty of trouble. Lea, less aggressive, usually just buys ice cream.

They're good friends, even if they occasionally abandon you for gushy romantic talk and girl sex. You tell yourself that as you stand against your wall, trying to resist indulging in stupid daydreams, like looking up and meeting eyes with some kind, mysterious new student across the room.

Hating yourself, you look across the room anyway, and you do meet someone's eyes: Lea.

Something's wrong.

Lea, like most faeries, loves glamour, is always trying to master her control of it. She has the minor changes down, but the more she tries to hide, the more the air around her shimmers, like a mirage. The air around her now is gold, and rippling like pond water. Her brown eyes are wide and panicked.

You're crossing the room before you realize you left

your shoes and purse behind. "What—"

"Not here," Lea says, and drags you away, out of the gym. Her hand is cold and wet.

She pulls you to the baseball field, far away from anyone. There's no light out here save the moon, and your bare feet are freezing. "Seriously," you say, walking by third base. "Lea, you're kind of freaking me—"

You stop. She lets go of your hand.

The dugout is encircled in salt. Riley paces back and forth inside, hissing words you can't understand. There's a smear of red across her mouth. Her eyes are red, too.

Riley is an oracle. This isn't Riley. This is something *wearing* Riley, something hiding between her skin and bones.

You look at Lea, and she's no longer shimmering. Her fluffy, white ballerina dress is torn and covered in too much blood. It's on her shoes and knees and hands.

There's blood on your hand too.

THINGS YOU DON'T KNOW:

- Whose blood is on your hand?
- How the hell did Riley get possessed buying a soda?
- What the fuck does Lea think *you* can do about it?

"Jesus, Lea, are you okay? We need to get you—you need a hospital, you—"

"I'm okay," Lea says, and she doesn't *sound* hurt, despite all evidence to the contrary. "It's not me, not mine."

"But who—" You jump when Riley slams her hands into the metal fence. "We have to call the cops," you say. "We have—"

"We can't."

"They've got people for this," you insist, because they must. Mrs. MacReady who ran the deli got possessed, what, four years ago? She killed her baby, and her husband called 911, and somehow they were able to pull the demon out. Your second-grade teacher got possessed too, but better not bring that up. He didn't survive the exorcism.

Riley will, though. Riley's strong: she takes kickboxing classes, and can actually do a pull-up, and was the only one on the aquarium field trip who ate at Teddy's Tex-Mex and didn't suffer brutal food poisoning. Once you go to the cops—

"We can't," Lea says again, and drags you to the bleachers. There's a body underneath, although it doesn't really look like a person anymore. It looks like...laundry, a big pile of it, red and shapeless and soaking wet. Your brain doesn't want to see it, keeps trying to puzzle it out: who would leave all these rags here? Why do they smell so *bad*?

You blink, and the rags give way to flesh, piles and piles of discarded meat. There's no frame, no bones. Where— where are the *bones*?

"It's Carter," Lea says, and you stare at her.

"How can you—"

"The necklace."

You turn back and spot the dark cross in the middle of

human goop. There's only one person in the whole school who wears such a large and laughably inaccurate statement of abstinence: Carter Laughton. You've never liked Carter; he's rich and wears endless sweater vests and actually thinks student council is important, but. Jesus. Nobody deserves this.

Carter and Riley used to date, way back in freshman year, some kind of weird, opposites attract thing. It ended when Riley caught Carter making out with some cheerleader and promptly set his backpack on fire. But that was *ages* ago, and anyway, it's obvious that Riley's possessed. The cops can't arrest her, not when she wasn't in control—

"Don't you remember Mrs. MacReady?" Lea asks.

"Yeah. And they exorcised her—"

"No, after."

After. Yes, you remember after. But that's not—

"Lea!" a voice singsongs. Riley, obviously, but her voice is wrong, uncharacteristically high-pitched. "I'm waaaiting!"

Lea inhales and brushes past you, and you really don't want to follow. You just want to go home, and when have you *ever* wanted that before? But you don't have a choice. You've been friends with Riley for three years, ever since she let you cheat on a math test you forgot to study for. And Lea, Lea's been your best friend since you were six and playing monsters at recess. She'd wanted to become a centaur then, and you did, too, because you wanted whatever Lea wanted.

There's no choice but to follow.

THINGS YOU KNOW:

- Nobody pressed charges against Mrs. MacReady, but the whole town turned against her. "Not my child," people said, refusing to sell her food, stamps, gasoline. "I'd have fought harder, if it'd been my child." Even your *asshole werewolf father* said this, and the thing is, he meant it.
- Mrs. MacReady drowned in her bathtub after swallowing an entire bottle of expired Vicodin. No note. None needed.
- You don't want Riley to die.
- You don't want Lea to die.
- You don't want to die.
- This isn't going to end well for anybody.

Riley's eyes are still red, but you wouldn't be fooled even if they were brown; nothing sane, nothing human, smiles like that. Her blood-spattered skin seems pale in the moonlight, and there's some kind of white dust on her mouth and fingers. "B, you made it!"

"Riley," you say, which is a mistake. This isn't Riley. "What do you want?"

"Oh," Riley says. "Destruction, dismemberment." She grins wider, and you see some of her teeth are cracked. "Bones."

You think about the pile of red laundry that used to be

Carter, the white dust around Riley's mouth, and suppose you can add one more bullet point to the Things You Know.

Riley laughs, like she knows what you're thinking. Probably does. Lea teases you about your lists, but Riley never has, and you figure it's not a coincidence that you guys never hang out at her house, either. "Oh, B. Always trying to classify things, keep them in order. Make sense of this senseless world." She shakes her head. "Tonight must suck for you."

"Riley," Lea says, stepping closer. "I know you're in there somewhere—"

"Oh, are we at this part already?" Riley claps her hands and leans forward, eyes trailing up and down Lea's thin arms, her slim shoulders. Her prominent, exposed collarbone.

"Riley, it doesn't matter what you did," Lea says. Her voice is unsteady, her green wings fluttering uselessly behind her. "I know you didn't mean to. I know, and I love you. You can defeat this, Riley. You—"

"Wow," Riley says. "That was *terrible*. You'll have to try harder than that, if you wanna save Riley through the Power of Love." She turns to you, now eyeing your limbs, your big Norse bones. "B, I know *you* didn't sign off on this plan. *The Wrinkle in Time* is bullshit, remember?"

You're shaking, and it's not just the cold autumn night or your bare feet in the damp grass. "Stop it."

"Why? I'm not telling you anything you don't already know. Love can't save anyone in real life, remember? Love is the thing that keeps you prisoner. Love is the thing that breaks your bones. Love, and the light of the moon." Riley looks up at the sky. "How long has she been trying to save him with love, B? Only thing she needs is a silver bullet. You must have imagined it, shooting him. You'd be free. Don't you want to be free?"

You have, and you do. But he's still your father, even if he's an asshole, even if he's why your amazing, battle maiden mother is always apologizing or why you had to find a dress with long sleeves. He's your father, and your mother isn't the only one who loves him, because sometimes he loves you, too, because not every day is the full moon.

Freedom isn't a silver bullet. Freedom isn't even wings. Freedom is your feet, and the welcoming blue of the cold, patient sea.

But you don't want to die right now, not at the hands of your friend and in a stupid dress that makes you look like a giant blueberry.

"We have to call 911. We can't fix this, Lea."

Lea shakes her head. "They'll—she'll—"

"Die," Riley says happily. "You know how many hosts die during exorcisms? It's pretty ugly, B. You should look at the statistics. Even if Riley did survive, let's face it: she's not exactly a good girl. All this black, all these piercings. The fights, the mouthing off, the backpack incident. Be honest: didn't she all but invite me in?"

"Riley didn't—"

"Are you sure? She gets so mad sometimes, doesn't she? It's delicious, her fury. She wanted to become something powerful, some kind of avenger, and instead she can only wait for what's to come. Funny she didn't predict this. Funny she didn't do anything to stop it."

"That's not how being an oracle works," you say, angry at yourself for arguing, and arguing anyway.

"Convenient," Riley says, grinning. "You think anyone will buy that? People only know what they want to know, and it'll comfort them, believing that this only happens to other people, weak people, people who ask for it—"

"Riley didn't ask for it," Lea says. Her voice is steadier now. "Riley isn't weak. You're not, Riley. You've never been. You fight everything: jocks, internet trolls, sanctimonious calorie counters and gluten haters. You can fight this, too; I know you can. You can knock this asshole demon into next week."

"Now, Lea. Haven't we already—"

But Lea doesn't stop. "Fight your way free," she says, "and come back to me, cause we're gonna have the most awesome life. We're going to graduate and go to college and skinny dip our way through the Great Lakes. You'll major in depressing poetry and write creepy kids books, and I'll dance for Beyoncé; I'll dance on *Broadway*. You'll wear black at the wedding, just to piss off your mom, and we'll get married under the stars. And someday, when we're ready, we'll adopt cute Blasian babies: three of them, and we'll name them after your grandmother and my grandmother and Hermione Granger."

Riley's face twists, her fingers tightening on the chain link fence. Her eyes melt from red to dark brown to red again. "I don't, I can't—"

"You can," Lea says. She's crying, and Riley's crying,

and you're crying, too, uselessly in the background. "You can."

"Lea, I—"

"See that future, Riley, and cut a bitch to make it happen, because I love you. I love you."

The red bleeds out of Riley's eyes. "I love you, too," she says, and then her whole body is thrown across the dugout, back and forth, slamming into the fence. She screams, or roars; it's wordless defiance, hanging in the air, before she collapses on the ground.

For a long moment, no one moves.

Then Lea reaches forward, and her knee breaks the line of salt. You open your mouth, but Riley's already lifting her head, and you freeze. Hold your breath.

Her eyes are brown.

"Riley?"

Riley shudders. "You bet your sweet fairy ass." Her voice is thick with tears, robbed of her usual sass, but Lea laughs anyway, hugging Riley for all her worth.

You release your breath and walk forward, trying to stop shaking, trying to think. *It's over. It's over.*

In the distance, somebody screams. *Who—*

"You know," Riley says, suddenly clear. "I've never had fairy bones before. What do you taste like, I wonder?"

She lifts her head, and her eyes are still brown, but she's smiling, and *Oh Christ—*

Lea tries to scramble back, but Riley has too good a grip on her wing, twisting it backward until there's a sharp, cracking sound. Lea screams, and you're there, pulling her away. "Run!" you yell, and then you're punched so hard you feel like there's a hole in your chest.

You look down. Lea gasps. Riley withdraws her hand.

"Oh," you try to say, but can't, because there's an actual hole in your chest.

THINGS YOU KNOW:

- You're lying flat on your back, staring up at the sky. You don't remember falling, but there you are, listening to sirens, facing the moon. The sirens are strange because you never called 911, but the moon, the moon you understand. You always figured you'd die on the full moon.
- No. You never really thought you'd die at all.
- People shouldn't die on baseball fields. They shouldn't die in bare feet, or before they finish their homework, or graduate, or see France, or live.
- There's too much blood outside you. Was it really all inside you once? You don't know how. You don't know. That belongs on another list, but everything's muddling together now, blending, blurring. Maybe your lists are bleeding too.
- You're cold. You're cold. You're

There's no moon when you wake up. There's no light at all, actually, but you're still on your back; you don't know where. You can't see a thing.

You feel around, try not to panic. There are walls at both sides, enclosing you. You can't even sit up because you hit your head on something. A ceiling. A very low ceiling. A lid.

The last thing you remember, you were dying.

Shit.

THINGS YOU KNOW:

- You're in a coffin.
- Either you were prematurely buried (unlikely), or you finally became something after all.

Turns out, you're a revenant. Exactly what kind, you're not sure. No craving for brains, so not a zombie. No craving for blood, so not a vampire. It turns out you don't need to eat at all, actually, although you still do because old habits die hard. Probably why you make yourself breathe, too, anytime you catch your body forgetting to bother.

You died last week. Three days ago, you rose from your grave, breaking through your coffin and climbing through six feet of wet earth. Your parents took the news pretty well, all things considered. Your father even wept, squeezing you tight and crying into your muddy, blonde hair. This morning he made your favorite: chocolate chip pancakes.

You keep catching yourself thinking, *Maybe it'll be better, now that he's buried a child. Maybe he'll raise his fist and remember.*

Hope is the worst. It's what's been breaking your mother's heart for years, but a week ago you were dead. How can you turn your back on miracles now?

Turns out, you're the only one who feels this way.

THINGS YOU KNOW:

- Kat Lopez is the Sheriff's daughter, and also a banshee. On their way to the dance, her girlfriend rear-ended another car because Kat freaked her out by suddenly screaming. She called the Sheriff, who put his deputies on alert, and ended up giving the couple a ride. Kat had barely gotten out of the car when she screamed again, this time for you.
- The Sheriff is the one who managed to stop the demon from eating your bones. He also saved Lea, and captured Riley alive. You should probably get him a card or something.
- There aren't nearly enough state sanctioned exorcists for how many demonic possessions occur per state. Riley could be waiting weeks for her exorcism, if it works at all. The demon was telling the truth: the stats *are* ugly.
- It was also telling the truth about people: they only know what they want to know.

Your mom eventually lets you leave the house, although she insists you take one of her swords. You end up wearing a trench coat to hide it. You're not sure if it's illegal for underage revenants to carry swords around town, but it *sounds* illegal.

You walk to Lea's and endure hugs from her parents, grandparents, and brothers before finally escaping. Lea's on her bed, staring blankly at photo albums, wearing the Tinkerbell pajamas you bought for her becoming gift. The air around her shimmers gold. You don't call her on it.

"I got you something," Lea says. She can't meet your eyes, and that scares you for some reason. "I didn't think you'd have a becoming party, but. Call it a Happy Resurrection gift. A Sorry My Girlfriend Killed You gift. A Sorry I Was Stupid And Got You Killed gift."

You don't know what to say to that, so you just open the bag. It's *Night of the Living Dead* pajamas.

"Inaccurate," you tell her, "but totally awesome."

You end up staying the night. Eventually, Lea lets the glamour fade, and you see the heavy bags under her eyes, the black bruises on her brown skin and her broken left wing, healing in a cast. You sign your full name in tiny, red letters.

"Are they letting you see her?" you ask, stealing a spoonful of Ben & Jerry's. Lea doesn't look up, and it takes you a minute to realize why. "But...after the exorcism, you'll see her then, right?"

"She killed you."

"No, she didn't."

"She *killed you*. You were dead, B. You came back, but—"

"The demon killed me," you say. "That wasn't Riley. You know that."

Lea stabs her ice cream, eyes distant. "I know Riley didn't invite it in, not on purpose. But...people can fight them off. I read some survivors' accounts, and you just have to want it enough. You just have to fight hard, and...she didn't love me enough, B. She didn't love us enough to save us."

Lea finally looks up, eyes dark and jaw set, and you want to say something; you want so hard to say something because you know, you *know* she's wrong, but all the words are jumbled up inside you. Your body feels heavy under their weight.

"Riley killed my best friend," Lea says, "and I can't forgive her for that. Not ever."

In the end, you don't say anything; you just lie by her side, silently watching Disney movies until she falls asleep, because that's what she needs from you. You never fall asleep, though. You haven't slept since you died. In the morning, you go home, and make breakfast for yourself. You accidentally leave a syrup smear on the counter, and your father, already stewing for one reason or another, brushes up against it. He howls, rips off the stained shirt, and backhands you across the face.

It doesn't hurt, not really. Not your face, anyway.

THINGS YOU KNOW:

- What your mother will say later: "It was my fault, arguing last night." Or: "He's just been so stressed, with everything that's happened." Or: "It's the werewolf in him, honey. Don't ever forget he loves you." Or: "You deserve so much more than me. I'm sorry I'm sorry I'm sorry."
- The full moon is still weeks away.
- Your father is a werewolf, but mostly he's just an asshole because the Sheriff is also a werewolf, and Kat Lopez never comes to school in long sleeves.
- Every day is the full moon, or has the potential to be.

THINGS YOU DON'T KNOW:

- If you can't sleep, or just don't need to, if the dead can walk and talk but never dream.
- How to convince Lea that she's wrong, that everyone's wrong about Riley.
- How to save Riley if love isn't enough.

THINGS YOU HOPE:

- Maybe, just maybe, it is.

Sheriff Lopez isn't happy to see you or your trench coat, though he does say thank you for the card. He makes you repeat the visitation rules at least twenty times. "I know you want to save your friend," he says, "but that may not be possible."

You know that. You also know there's more than one way to save somebody.

The demon wearing Riley is sitting cross-legged on the floor. It claps her hands while you sit down across from them, salt and iron between you. "They told me you came back," the demon says, "but *brava*, B. Look at you, all grown up. A monster, just like the rest of us."

"Hey, Riley."

"Still have that little love tap we gave you?"

You do. The hole is just above your boobs, stuffed with cotton and taped shut, effectively making you an undead teddy bear. Riley would think that was hilarious. "I wanted to say I'm sorry."

The demon raises Riley's eyebrow. "I kill you, and you apologize for it? Apple really doesn't fall far from the tree."

That stings, but you ignore it. "That night on the field, I was talking to the demon instead of you. I shouldn't have done that, Riley, should never have called it your name. I'm only going to talk to you now, okay?"

"Sounds like a pretty one-sided conversation."

"Yeah," you say. "I know you probably won't be able to talk back, and that's okay. You can still hear me, and I need to say some things, things that other people should be saying, that Lea doesn't know and maybe you don't know, but that *I* know."

The demon snorts. "You're going to read me your list?"
"Yeah," you say. "This is my list, Ri."

THINGS I KNOW:

- You can't make a person do whatever you want
just because you love them. And a person can't
do whatever you want just because they love
you. Love isn't magic, and it isn't big speeches or
swelling music or miracles, either. Love is
constancy, dependability. Love is not love which
alters when it alteration finds.

- Love isn't always healthy. Sometimes, love is
broken bones. Sometimes, it's not worth fighting
for. But you can't decide that for other people.
You can only be ready when they decide it for
themselves.

- You didn't ask for this, Riley. You don't deserve
what's happened to you. It doesn't matter how
many fights you've been in or how you dress.
That's a lie they tell, that they have a type, that
the people imprisoned are responsible for their
imprisonment. Monsters can happen to anyone.
You have nothing to apologize for.

- You're scared, you're hurt, and you're lonely.
Maybe you're still fighting, and just can't get free,
or maybe you think the best thing you can do is
appease it, try not to make it angrier. I wish I had
the answers for you, but I don't. I can't exorcise
you, Ri.

- This is what I can do: I can sit here and remind you that you're not the monster, you're not the demon, you're not the asshole, or the creature of the moon. I'm just going to sit here and keep reminding you until you're ready to hear it, until you can come out and tell me you understand. Cause I'm scared, Riley. I think Mrs. MacReady must have forgotten who the real monster was, and my teacher, I don't know if he knew; I think maybe he just didn't want to survive the exorcism. Sometimes my mom says I'd be better off without her, and it scares me so much, I think…I just don't want to lose you. I refuse to lose you.
- You're my friend, Riley. I love you, and you sure as hell are worth fighting for.

You talk to Riley for about an hour before going home to pack. The demon taunts you, of course, laughs at you for thinking you can help at all, and maybe you can't, but love is about the trying, not the results. You'll go back tomorrow.

Your mom looks at the red mark on your cheek and hugs you. "This is my fault," she says. "I'm sorry, I'm sorry, I'm sorry."

Gently, you pull away.

"I talked to Lea's parents. They said I could stay there. I've always said no before, but…I'm going, and. You could come with me, if you want?"

Your mother buries her face in her hands and cries.

You swallow, because you knew that would be her answer, even if you hoped otherwise. It's okay. It hurts, but it's okay.

Try again tomorrow.

"We'll figure it out together," you say, kissing your mother on the forehead. "When you're finally ready, we'll make it work without him."

You don't say goodbye to your father. Some things aren't worth fighting for, even if you love them, even if they love you. You won't turn your back on miracles, but sometimes enough is fucking enough.

THINGS YOU DON'T KNOW:

- Will your mom ever leave your father? Will Riley survive the exorcism? Will she and Lea fix what's broken between them?
- Are you a draugr, maybe, or a different, less Nordic species of undead? You've been doing research on Wikipedia, since sleeping isn't your thing anymore. You think of your grave sometimes, and shudder, overcome with dread. Is this a clue to who you are, or just a sign of PTSD?
- Were you always meant to be undead, or were you supposed to become something else? Did another destiny once await you?
- Would you just sink, if you walked into the ocean now? Would you sit there forever, alone at the bottom of the cold, patient sea?

THINGS YOU KNOW:

- Dying sucks. It's not freedom at all. Fuck that sea.

  _____

SPIDER
SEASON
FIRE
SEASON

SPIDER SEASON, FIRE SEASON

I. Spider Season

The house is haunted, of course[1]. That's why the rent is so cheap. It doesn't matter that it's only April, that ghosts dream quietly when the world is in full bloom. Nearly any haunting will be small: flickering lights, a mysterious lullaby, an intrusive thought chasing the living from room to room. Fatalities are incredibly rare, though most people, even the disbelievers, fail to find that reassuring.

December is not most people, not when it comes to the dead, but she promised herself twenty years ago: *when I'm grown up, when I can choose, I'll never live with a ghost again.*

Unfortunately, part of adulthood is discovering you can't always afford better choices. Especially when a child is growing inside you. Especially when someone is hunting you both.

1. Spiders, stalking, violence, murder, child death, intimate partner abuse, abusive language.

The house is white and sprawling and isolated, a short distance from the Mendocino Coast. There are more spiders than ghosts her first week there, all seeking shelter from the rain. December finds them on walls, in her bedsheets, curling up inside her shoes. She talks to them often, names them, wonders what they might name her in return. It's always best to befriend house spiders, something she learned when she was young. Dozens might be crawling around at any time; more, if you're counting the dead ones.

The human ghost in this house is Olivia de la Cuesta, murdered five years ago in a botched home invasion. By all accounts, she was bright and ambitious, two months shy of leaving for her freshman year at college. December lives in the house two weeks before Olivia's nightmare begins to manifest visibly: wet footprints, all over the hardwood floor. When she steps in them, December can feel sand between her toes.

Sometimes, there is music: Ellie Goulding, slurred and strange.

Sometimes, December brushes her teeth and spits out Olivia's blood instead of toothpaste.

It's not a restful environment, certainly not ideal for a woman eight months pregnant. December will have to be vigilant, although it's unlikely Olivia will be capable of any real harm until she manifests at her full strength, when the days are darker and the nights are longer, when spirits are at both their most dangerous and most coherent. Ghosts are tricky in winter. To be dead is to be disoriented, but if December can establish contact in the next few months, if she can slowly, repetitively, build trust between them, then she just might wake Olivia up by the new year. They could all live together safely. Maybe even happily.

But it's always a risk, depending on others for happiness, the living as much as the dead. If you need someone to follow, they'll stay behind. If you need them to stay behind, they'll follow. They'll never let go.

Another contraction. Braxton-Hicks: false labor, real pain. December eases herself down on the couch, as she feels a small, dark spider crawl across her bare feet. "What should I call you?" she asks the spider. The baby's name, of course, she already knows.

He won't find us here, December promises her child, but this is a lie: it's only a matter of time.

II. Beach Season

She wakes up in the dark, too quickly, a dream still spun about her. Where is she? What is she doing here? There was laughter, she remembers that. There was blood everywhere, bright red and gushing. What's happening, where is she, where—

Her bedroom. Of course, it was just a nightmare. It's okay, she's safe. Maybe still a little drunk: her skin feels strange, her head heavy. Her feet are still damp and dirty from the beach. She'd locked the door behind her, changed out of her jeans, forced herself to drink a glass of water— but the prospect of showering had been just too much. Standing was *effort*. So was taking off her hoodie or brushing her wind-tangled hair. She'd needed the relief of horizontality.

It's still so very dark out. She couldn't have slept for long.

There's music: "Ex's and Oh's" playing from the vicinity of her pillow. Groaning, she pushes the earbuds away, fumbling for her phone, and dropping it at the sound of footsteps down the hall.

There's someone in the house.

Her parents are out of town. Could they have come back early? They've basically been a wreck since finally accepting that no, she isn't going to live in this house forever; she's getting her degree in bioengineering, and then she's going to see the world. They could've come home—but that would be a waste of money, and Mama never wastes money already spent. No, it must have been her imagination. There's no one here, it was only a dream, there's no one—

The footsteps are louder. Voices, too. A man, laughing.

He's right outside her bedroom door.

She stops breathing. (Was she breathing before? She can't remember, she can't think, everything *hurts*.) There's a hand on the door, pushing it open—but it stops, as someone else calls out. Footsteps again, walking away, leaving her bedroom door half open.

Slowly, she slides out of bed, wincing at the chill of the hardwood floor. She has to get out of here. There's barely any space to hide in her closet, no room at all under her bed. If the man comes back, if he sees her…but the window, it always sticks, impossibly loud in the dark of night.

They'll catch her, whoever they are. They'll grab her by the ankles and pull her, screaming, back inside.

The back door. It's the only way.

She slips out of her bedroom carefully, eyes still not fully adjusted to the dark. She can't see the men, but can they see her? Are they watching her, even now? She creeps down the hall in slow motion, inching past the guest room, past the baby that woke her with their incessant screams—

Wait. Baby?

There's no baby; it was laughter that woke her, a man, two men, intruders, thieves—

But there *is* a baby, white and chubby and wailing her cute little head off. She can't be more than a couple months old. What is she doing here? Who put this nursery in her house? When did they do it, how, what the fuck is even *happening*—

"Olivia, sweetheart. Can you step away from the crib, please?"

Olivia looks up, heart in her throat. (*Something* is in her throat, something wrong; she's choking.) The man is there, the tall white man with the gun, he's laughing, he's laughing, he's *laughing*—

"I won't hurt you, Olivia. No one can anymore."

The man is gone. It's just a woman now, in her late twenties or early thirties. Dark frizzy hair, pale skin, a soft, sagging belly underneath a sleep-wrinkled tank top. "I don't suppose you remember me yet," the woman says. "I'm December, and that's Clara. We've done this a few times now."

The lights are on (when did the lights turn on),

flickering violently. Olivia doesn't understand; she doesn't understand any of this.

"You're dead, Olivia," December says softly. "You're dead and dreaming."

No. No. That doesn't make any sense. She was just at the beach a few hours ago with her friends, one last party before the future beckons them forward, drives them apart, swallows them whole. She was just in bed, dreaming of terrors, but she isn't, she can't be—

The men are still in the house. She can hear their footsteps. She has to get out.

"I know you're afraid," December says, "but I will wake you, I promise. I can help. We—" She closes her eyes. "We can be friends."

She says it like it's an inevitability, like something she desperately wishes wasn't true. But Olivia isn't fooled; she knows who her friends are. One of them lives only a few blocks away. If she can get to the back door, if she can escape—

But suddenly she's at the back door, pulling it open, and the man grabs her from behind, dragging her away. His breath smells like red wine and tobacco. He's laughing in her face.

She's fighting back, kicking and screaming. She has to get out of here; her parents need her to survive. She's punching and clawing, digging at his face. His cheek is bleeding. He isn't laughing anymore.

The gun is cold, kissing the hollow of her throat.

Olivia can't get out. She'll never get out.

III. Fire Season

It used to be scary in the closet. It was dark there, cold and quiet, and there was nothing to eat or drink at all. Clara slept curled up against her shoes. And it smelled, too, because she had to pee, and there was nowhere to go, so she went in her pants. Father would be mad, if he knew, but he doesn't because he hasn't unlocked the door yet. *You have to hide*, he'd whispered, so very long ago now. *I'll come back. I'll get you when it's safe.*

She doesn't know how long it's been. There's no time in the closet.

It's not so bad anymore, though, because she has a human friend, Dot. Dot is nine, just two years older than Clara, and she talks and dresses funny because she's from the future. Dot teaches Clara new songs they can sing, and Clara teaches Dot that spiders aren't scary, not even the ones that vanish when you blink. Clara tells Dot all her spider friends' names. Dot tells Clara that she's dead.

Clara doesn't mind being dead, exactly, but it's confusing sometimes. Other children have told her ghost stories before, sad souls who've been barred from the Kingdom of Heaven. Is that where Father is, the Kingdom of Heaven? But she has to wait for him; she promised she would, and anyway, he locked the door. She can't get out.

You can, Dot keeps telling her. The door is open, see?

But she doesn't see. With Dot's help, Clara has learned

to do magic: she can imagine the closet brighter and prettier and make it smell nicer, too—but the door is always shut. Only one person can open it. Clara knows this, the way she knows God exists, the way she knows the sun still rises and sets. She knows this because it's always been true.

Something's different today, though. The closet smells like smoke, no matter how hard Clara wishes it away, and it's hot in here, so hot. Dot's kneeling beside her, wearing that funny red sack she calls a backpack. Her eyes are watering, red and frightened.

"Clara," Dot says, "There's a really big wildfire. It moved so fast; it's already here. You have to come with me, okay?"

Why does Dot keep saying that? Can't she see the door is locked?

"The door is open, Clara!" Dot screams. "How did I get inside, if the door is shut?"

Clara doesn't know that. Maybe Dot isn't here. Maybe she's been the ghost all along.

Dot grabs Clara's hands. For a second, for just a second, they touch. That's never happened before, but Dot doesn't smile. She's coughing too hard. "You have to wake up now," Dot says, in between choking. "You can't wait anymore. If the house burns up, you'll burn up with it."

But Father—

"He's been dead for decades! He isn't coming back! Please, Clara." Dot starts crying. "You're my best friend."

Dot is Clara's best friend, too, and she doesn't like it when her friends are sad. But Dot's wrong this time. Clara can't leave the closet. It's the only place that's safe.

Then Dot disappears in the smoke. Clara hears her screaming from far, far away. "Let me go; I can't leave her! Clara, you have to follow me! Follow me!"

The closet is on fire now. But Father's coming; he'll open the door soon.

IV. Ghost Season

It takes too long, far too long, but finally, Jacob finds her.

She's come back to California, her first mistake, staying in some shithouse cottage by the coast. Dorothea grew up somewhere in this state, called herself a child of specters and the Santa Ana winds. She was always saying weird shit like that, at least before he trained her to speak like a person. Painstakingly, he'd taught her, molded her, protected and perfected her. Good wives were investments. You had to put in the work.

Jacob might have expected some goddamn gratitude. Instead, Dorothea fled with his unborn baby, grabbing her red backpack and vanishing in the night. He'd never liked that backpack. Her eyes shifted suspiciously whenever he brought it up. *I've always kept a go-bag,* she'd whined, when he'd told her to throw it away. *Fire moves fast. You have to be ready.*

She thinks she's ready. That bitch. That whore. She has no fucking idea.

Fire will find her tonight.

Jacob walks through the house, pouring kerosene as he

goes. He'd watered the front lawn with it, too, the thick mist shrouding him from view. It's not raining, though, not even properly cold. Almost Christmas, and only forty degrees. How do you trust a state without seasons?

Silently, he steps into the nursery. His baby is sleeping in her crib, dressed in a Star Wars onesie, a head full of dark, curly hair. She looks like him. He'd suspected as much. Dorothea had wanted to name her Clara, but Jacob's already decided to call her Lucy. He'll teach Lucy manners. He'll teach her respect. She won't grow up believing in nonsense like ghosts.

Dorothea changed her name when she ran, cut and dyed her hair, too. It looks ugly, butch. And whoever heard of a name like December?

"It's all right now," Jacob whispers to Lucy, touching her cheek. "Daddy's gonna make it all better soon."

A spider runs across his finger.

He curses, flings it into the wall, but it vanishes before he can crush it for good. He stares at his hand. That's not possible; must have been some trick of the light. He rubs his knuckles against his jeans and leaves Lucy where she is, for now. He'll come back when he runs out of kerosene. If she's lucky, Dorothea won't even wake up before fire engulfs the house. He'll have to make sure she isn't lucky.

Jacob turns and startles hard. There's someone in the doorway, but it isn't Dorothea. Some Mexican teenager wearing glasses, an oversized gray hoodie, and boxer shorts. Jacob has never seen her before, even though he's been watching the house for the past week. Is she some kind of live-in nanny? Illegal, probably, watching Lucy for a few bucks while Dorothea sleeps like a lazy cow.

It doesn't matter. She's seen his face now. She has to go.

"I won't hurt you," Jacob lies. "You understand?"

She stares at him, eyes wide with terror.

"Yeah, I didn't think so." He reaches slowly into his jacket, a comforting smile on his face. "Come here, bitch. I'll make it quick."

But the girl bolts.

Swearing, Jacob drops the open jug of kerosene and runs after her. She's quick, already at the backdoor, but he gets her by the hood and yanks backwards, hard. She screams and stumbles, clawing at his face, but her fingers won't seem to connect with his skin. He slams her to the floor, pulling out his gun and jamming the muzzle into her throat. Blood wells, then spurts, gushing out of her neck—but he hasn't pulled the trigger yet. What *is* this, what—

And then there's a sound behind him, and it's Dorothea, swinging a Maglite at his face.

His nose erupts in blood as the bone crunches. "Fuck!" Jacob screams, dropping the gun.

Dorothea has Lucy strapped to her stomach. The go-bag hangs loosely off one shoulder. "Go, Olivia!" she yells, swinging the Maglite again; it catches Jacob against the left temple, and he drops to his knees. "You can, I promise you can!"

Blood drips into Jacob's eyes. He sees the Mexican girl through it, but she's just…standing there, in the open doorway, staring out at the backyard. Maybe she's having one of those absence seizures; maybe all the blood is some weird medical condition, hemophiliacs or something. It doesn't matter; if she wants to play lamb for the slaughter, so much the better.

Dorothea reaches for the gun, another mistake, and Jacob tackles her at the knees. She falls backwards, trying to catch herself with one arm while protecting Lucy with the other. Her head bounces against the hardwood floor. Her eyes flutter, roll back.

Jacob kneels over her. His blood drips against her check. "I told you," he says. "You don't walk out on me. You can't take what's mine and expect to escape retribution."

She blinks, too slow. He's not sure she's really hearing him, and that won't do. He flicks his lighter on and off. "Wake up, Dorothea."

Her eyes blink, again and again. Finally, they focus. "Jacob," she whispers.

Jacob smiles and throws the lighter.

Dorothea struggles frantically as the hallway erupts in flames, trying to kick, to shove him off. It's all too easy to hold her down. The baby carrier, though, is a problem. Lucy is still trapped inside it, red-faced and screaming. How the hell is he supposed to get her out of this thing?

Dorothea begins hyperventilating as the smoke thickens. "Jacob," she begs, choking out the words. "Please, please don't do this. You don't have to do this—"

"I told you," Jacob reminds her. "If only you'd listened—"

Something touches his ankle, then skitters up his calf.

He twists around, batting at his jeans. A spider crawls out, then another, then *dozens*, all spilling to the floor.

"The *fuck*," Jacob yells, frantically brushing them away —but there are more of them, too many, crawling across his shirt, whispering up his back. One skitters across his cheek before he knocks it away. The spider disappears, and the ones on the floor—where are the ones on the floor? What, what is *happening*—

The front of the house is engulfed in flames. Dorothea runs past Jacob, swaying and unsteady; he lunges for her and misses, distracted by impossibility. The Mexican girl, Olivia, is still in the doorway, and Dorothea doesn't push past her; she runs straight *through* her.

It doesn't make sense. None of this makes sense.

The gun. The gun makes sense. He just needs to find it, somewhere in this smoke, but he can't, he can't find it anywhere—

Because it's in Olivia's hand.

She stares at it, turning it this way and that. She lifts her head, looks at him.

Suddenly, he's on the ground.

She's holding him down, which is impossible. She's a bundle of twigs, can't weigh more than a hundred pounds. Doesn't seem to weigh anything, and yet Jacob can't get up, no matter how hard he fights back, kicking and screaming. He has to get out of here. This is a madhouse, and it's burning down around him. He has to get out of here and drag his wife back in.

"Olivia!" Dorothea keeps yelling. "You have to wake up now! There's no more time. You have to follow me!"

Olivia stares at him. She presses the gun into the hollow of his throat.

"Olivia! Follow me!"

"You won't," Jacob says, swallowing against the gun. "You can't—"

Olivia starts laughing.

There are spiders crawling up her arms. There are tears in her eyes. She looks at the backdoor and *smiles*.

"I can," she says, wondering.

V. Earthquake Season

"Shhh," Mom says softly. "Wake up, sweetheart. You're just having a bad dream."

It was a very bad dream. The ground shook apart, swallowing Clara whole. She's not usually scared of earthquakes. They have little ones all the time—Mom says every season is earthquake season in California—but this was the Big One, and Clara didn't just die; she went *missing*. She kept dreaming and dreaming, and nobody found her ghost.

"Impossible," Olivia says, perched on Clara's bed. Her neck is all bloody—it usually is, at night—but she says it doesn't hurt anymore. "We'd find your ghost anywhere."

"Promise?" Clara asks.

"Promise."

"*Pinky* promise?"

Mom and Olivia solemnly pinky promise.

A pinky promise can't be broken. Clara knows that, like she knows the sky is blue, like she knows that any bad dream can be broken eventually, if you try hard enough. But still… "Mom? What if you die like Olivia?"

"Then," Mom says, brushing Clara's hair away from her forehead, "you and Olivia can wake me."

Clara nods sleepily. That makes sense. She sinks back down in bed, giggling at the tickling between her toes. "Okay," she announces seriously. "I'm ready to sleep now."

The spiders sleep with her, dreaming of sweet and sticky things.

———————————————

SUCH LOVELY TEETH
SUCH BIG TEETH

SUCH LOVELY TEETH, SUCH BIG TEETH

AFTER, THEY MOVE. They[1] travel hours and hours away, and Mom says it'll be safer here, in their little blue house on Meadowbrook Lane. *No one will hurt you*, she says. *Not ever again, Reagan. You're safe.*

Only Mom doesn't know about the wolf that lives across the street. The wolf moves like a man, talks like a man, picks up the paper in his boxers and drinks coffee like a man.

But Reagan isn't fooled.

It's her third week in the third grade, and Reagan has to talk in front of the whole class. "My report," she says, "is on wolves. Wolves are very dangerous animals. They're attracted to little girls and the color red. They swallow their prey whole."

---

1. violence, trauma, murder of children, implied child sexual abuse, blood/gore, gaslighting.

There's a parent-teacher conference that day.

She meets Dr. McGinnis the next week.

Dr. McGinnis doesn't have a stethoscope. She has a notebook instead, and she writes in it whenever Reagan says something wrong. "Can you tell me what it's like, being swallowed whole?"

Reagan doesn't like to talk about that.

"It's bad," she says finally. "It's dark and wet, wet all over."

"And what about the man, the man that hurt you?"

"He wasn't a man," Reagan says.

Dr. McGinnis writes that down.

The wolf on Meadowbrook Lane hosts the neighborhood Christmas party.

Reagan screams as Mom pries her away from the bed and roughly pulls a green dress with a big, green bow over her head. She doesn't have any red clothes anymore, not after burning her sweater in the bathtub and accidentally melting the shower curtain into oozing, pink plastic. "Please, baby," Mom begs. "Dr. McGinnis says this is important. It's been months since we moved here, and you haven't—you have to learn to socialize normally."

That doesn't mean anything to Reagan. Mom tugs at her wrist, dragging her from the room, so she bites Mom's fingers, hard.

Mom might have yelled once, but now she starts crying. Mom cries a lot these days. "Baby, it's okay," she says, kneeling and pulling Reagan in close. "It—it was too far to go on your own, I should never have let you—but I'm here now, okay? I'm here."

Mom apologizes a lot and makes promises she can't keep. She can't protect Reagan from wolves when she doesn't even *believe* in wolves. Reagan misses her grandma. Her grandma was there, in the dark. Her grandma knows what's out there.

Reagan misses the man with the axe, too.

"We don't have to stay long," Mom says, standing. "Just for a little while. Maybe you'll even make some friends!"

Reagan used to have friends. That didn't stop her from being eaten.

The wolf has pale eyes and a scruffy chin, and he's wearing a Santa hat on his head. He crouches down in front of Reagan, smiling so thinly she can't get a good look at the size of his teeth. "Does the little lady want something to eat?"

Reagan steps back.

"Please forgive her," Mom says. "She's…shy. She's been through a lot."

The wolf looks at Reagan. He sniffs and his eyes widen; he is silent for a heartbeat, and she doesn't know how to read his face. Can he smell the other wolf on her? Does she still stink of his stomach juices? But then he smiles at Mom and stands. "No problem," he says, glancing back down at her. "Maybe a little later, huh?"

He walks back to his other guests, mingling in the kitchen, and Mom turns and points to kids making a snowman in the backyard. Reagan refuses to join them. They wouldn't let her anyway—they call her weirdo all the time at school. Besides, she doesn't want to let the wolf out of her sight. His eyes wander, following children…but never the little girls.

Mostly, he leaves the kitchen to circle back to one boy, a big kid on the couch, maybe twelve or thirteen. He's wearing a red sweater and laughing at everything the wolf says.

"Reagan," Mom says. "What about him, over there?"

Reagan turns. It's Eric, halfway inside the coat closet, playing all by himself. She likes Eric: he's funny, and he's always reading, and he did his animal report on the Loch Ness Monster. Reagan's pretty sure he had a parent-teacher conference too, but she doesn't think he goes to any special doctors.

Eric's the only boy who isn't mean to her, *and* he has dinosaur toys. But—

"Go on," Mom says, and pushes Reagan forward.

Eric smiles when she sits down and gives her the Stegosaurus to play with. The Stegosaurus is the best. She attacks Eric's Apatosaurus and forgets to keep track of the wolf. Maybe she forgets on purpose. Sometimes it's easier to play dinosaurs than think about boys in red.

She still doesn't eat at the party. She has to wait forever, even after Eric and his dinosaurs have already gone home. Mom finally says they can go, and makes chicken strips for dinner. Reagan chews and chews and chews them until they are nothing but mush. She has to make sure they are dead. She has to make sure nothing comes back to life inside her.

A week later, the boy in red goes missing, and no one ever sees him again.

In the spring, Dr. McGinnis asks, "Reagan, what do *you* think happened to Jason Zeigler?"

She doesn't want to know, not really. She just wants Reagan to say all the right words. "Jason's daddy took him because he wasn't going to see Jason anymore because there was a divorce and stuff."

"What if a monster took him?"

"There aren't any monsters."

"Hm," Dr. McGinnis says, tapping her pen against her notebook. "Let's talk about the hunter."

"He saved me," Reagan says. "He's good."

Dr. McGinnis writes that down. She leans back in her chair, looking at Reagan like she's a thing that needs rearranging. "Do you still dream about wolves?"

Reagan doesn't, or not very often. She dreams about Grandma sometimes, rocking in her chair and murmuring words no one else understands. Mom says she's sick, and when Mom says sick, she means crazy, some kind of crazy that only old people get. Grandma lives in the nursing home now, far, far away with all the other old, crazy people. Reagan isn't allowed to see her.

"Sometimes, I dream about wolves," Reagan says. "They're really scary dreams. I cry, sometimes. But I don't dream about them as much as I used to."

Mostly Reagan dreams about the hunter, the man in the black hood and black half-mask who carried a bag of stones across his back and a bloodstained axe in each hand. He'd used those blades on the wolf's belly, carefully carving Reagan and her grandma out, and then placed the rocks where their bodies had been.

The newspeople call the hunter a dangerous vigilante. Reagan looks up the word. They think vigilante means murderer. She thinks it means a hero who kills, a hero with sharp teeth.

She decides not to tell Dr. McGinnis that, though.

The hunter keeps a blog, when he's not carving little girls and old women from the bellies of wolves. She finds it during summer break, when other kids are swimming or going to camp. *They call me a monster*, he writes. *But there are real monsters you should fear, killers that prey on children, creatures that can't be killed by ordinary means.* Rocks are very important, Reagan learns. You can cut a wolf down with an axe, but you can only keep him down with the heavy weight of stone.

Reagan spends all summer collecting rocks and hiding them around her room.

People leave messages for the hunter, calling him crazy or asking for help. The hunter rarely responds, but what else can she do?

Red Hoodie: Hunter, I've found one. He killed a boy last Christmas. Can you come? Please, will you come?

He doesn't come.

Grandma dies after Thanksgiving, only a week before Reagan's tenth birthday. Mom doesn't let her go to the funeral. Instead, she writes a report about magnets. Magnets are really boring, but she works hard on it anyway. She hasn't had a special parent-teacher conference since last year and that means Mom cries a lot less than she used to. If Reagan could make a friend, Mom might never cry again.

Reagan still doesn't really want friends. Most of the kids in her class are dumb. They care about stupid things and fear what can't actually hurt them and are repetitively, pointlessly cruel to one another. Eric's different, of course. He still gets into trouble sometimes because he reads about the wrong things at the wrong times, and he's always running late. But he's never mean to anyone, and he has all these freckles on his nose. Last month he made a special Valentine's Day card with dinosaurs on it just for her. Reagan finds herself watching him when she should be reading her book or listening to the teacher or thinking about wolves. She likes Eric. She likes him a lot.

But bad things happen when people get distracted,

when eyes are elsewhere and there's no one left to stand watch.

Reagan begins fifth grade, and things start changing. *She* starts changing.

First, it's her boobs. They aren't much to look at, but most girls in her class aren't even growing bumps yet. Mom buys her training bras in almost every color and Reagan pretends to be excited, but she's not, not about that. She *is* excited about her email. Finally, finally the hunter has written her back.

Hunter: Watch, but don't engage. Tell me if your wolf takes interest in one particular child. Will come when able.

Reagan reads it over and over, feeling safe for the first time in years. She has someone on her side, someone who knows. The hunter will come back and save her.

But that's when the dreams begin.

The hunter is there, standing above her. She's tied to the bed; she can't escape. The white sheets beneath her are covered in blood and clumps of fur, and her belly is split wide open. The hunter sets the stones inside her stomach. She sinks and sinks and sinks—

Reagan wakes up then, shaking. She rolls out of bed and examines herself in the mirror. Her teeth don't seem any bigger. Her ears are the same size too, but there's hair on her legs that shouldn't be there. She attacks it with scissors. In a week, it grows back.

She cuts it down again and goes to her computer. The

hunter's last entry was twelve days ago. It says only that the streets of Milwaukee will be safer that night. Milwaukee is a very long way away.

Reagan logs in. Red Hoodie: Hunter, how does someone BECOME a wolf?

The hunter doesn't respond.

There's a boy dressed up as a devil, and the wolf is touching him too much.

Reagan goes to all the holiday parties now, even if Mom has to work. She promised to keep an eye on the wolf, and she means to keep her promise, although sometimes her eye strays to Eric too—he's dressed up as a robot this year. She tries not to get distracted. This wolf is so much smarter than the one that swallowed her. For almost two years, she's seen nothing suspicious—he blends into the crowd, says all the right things. Children trust him with their secrets.

The devil-boy is telling him one right now.

Reagan isn't close enough to hear, but she knows what a secret looks like. The wolf nods, murmuring. His hand rests on the boy's back. The boy doesn't notice—the wolf's touch is familiar to him.

The boy is in trouble.

Reagan pulls out her cell phone, goes to the hunter's blog.

Red Hoodie: You have to come NOW.

When she looks up, the wolf is looking over the boy's shoulder, watching her.

She tries not to swallow, even as her fingers clutch tighter around the phone. This isn't the first time he's stared at her for a moment too long—Reagan thinks he knows what she's becoming, maybe knew even before she did. He doesn't know about the hunter, though. He can't know about that; he *can't*—

The wolf glances back down and smiles, reaching for the boy's face. His thumb hovers over the boy's lips, slowly brushing away invisible crumbs. Reagan takes a breath and looks back at her phone. There's a new blog post from the hunter.

Can't talk long. Police are on to me; have to run. May not make it. Never doubt: the wolves are real, they are out there, and they are coming for you.

Alone, in the middle of the wolf's house, Reagan tries very hard not to cry.

By Thanksgiving Break, the devil-boy is gone.

"How well did you know Aaron Parker?"

Reagan shrugs. "Not very. He was older than me, middle school. I guess he's run away a bunch of times before."

Dr. McGinnis nods. "You'll be in middle school next year," she says. "Sixth grade. Are you nervous?"

"A little."

"What else scares you, Reagan?"

This is the tricky part.

"Sometimes," Reagan says, "there are monsters in my

dreams. But they're just dreams, and I don't have very many anymore. The man who hurt me, he was a kind of monster, but really, he was a man. And he can't hurt me anymore."

Dr. McGinnis sets the notebook aside. "Reagan, I think you're making excellent progress."

She might be making progress in therapy, but outside of it, everything only gets worse.

Her period begins at the end of summer, dark red blood ruining her underwear and pajama pants and bedsheets. There's hair under her arms, on her legs, in *between* her legs, and it only grows back darker and thicker than before. Mom buys her tampons and razors and real bras, and tells her everything is fine. Everything is not fine. Reagan dreams of flesh and wakes up hungry. She dreams of stone and wakes up cold.

She gets taller, not very tall. Her hips get wider. Her boobs keep growing. They're uncomfortable and get in the way of everything, but boys seem to like them a lot. She sees them sometimes, looking at her, fingers twitching at their sides. She knows what they're thinking, how they want to touch her, all of her. Sometimes, she wants to touch them too, just to see what it feels like, to know if their skin is different from girl skin, if their lips are as soft as they look.

She thinks about touching Eric most of all.

Eric has gotten taller too, much taller than Reagan, but

his hips are narrow. His whole body is. He joins the swim team in November and Reagan goes to all the meets, even some of the practices, where she sneaks glances while hiding behind the stands. Eric glides through the water gracefully, like some kind of sea creature returning home.

She's not the only one watching him. The wolf is there too. The wolf is always there.

The wolf is the swim coach.

She tries hard not to know what she knows, but it becomes impossible to deny. This thing she's becoming…it stirs inside of her all the time now, at school, at home, alone in her bed with nothing but her hands in the dark to keep her company. She hates it; she's ashamed of it; it's *wrong*, but there her fingers are, on the inside of her thighs, and she explores, reaching, massaging what's inside her. She holds her breath as long as she can and shakes under the sheets.

She smells sweat and wet fur and barely gets to the bathroom before she vomits.

"Twelve years old," Dr. McGinnis says. "Almost a teenager. Do you have any plans?"

Reagan does. She's going to school. After, she'll wait until swim practice starts and watch the wolf watch Eric. Then she'll ride her bike home and eat cake for dinner. Mom said she'd try to leave work early, but she won't get home before ten; she never does. She'll text, though, probably apologize twice, and do something big this weekend to make up for it. Maybe they'll go to the beach. Reagan likes the beach, even when it's cold.

In her daydreams, the sweet ones, the ones that hurt the most, Reagan imagines asking Eric along. They could whisper secrets into seashells and chase each other across the sand and maybe, just maybe, he would forgive her for the terrible thing she was. He would even love her for it, the way he loves all strange things, the way he himself is strange. They could be strange and wonderful together.

But monsters cannot be wonderful, and monsters should not be loved, and Reagan doesn't know how to stop it. She doesn't know how to wish it all away.

"Nothing big," Reagan says and tries to mirror Dr. McGinnis's smile.

The wolf doesn't try anything at swim practice. It happens after, and by then, Reagan's too late.

She's heading to her bicycle when she sees it, Eric walking with the wolf to a car. Eric's dad isn't there. She doesn't know where he is, but he's not there, and Eric's opening the passenger door; he's getting inside, and the wolf is slipping behind the wheel.

Reagan yells but she's too far away. Eric doesn't hear

her. Neither does the wolf because, for a wolf, his ears are awfully small. The car pulls out of the parking lot and takes off, far faster than she can run. She runs anyway, though, pulling her helmet out of her backpack. She jumps up on her bicycle and pedals as fast as she can.

She can't catch the wolf, of course. The car's already turning on Main Street, driving long out of view. If he's taking Eric somewhere far away, somewhere secret, she'll never find them. But maybe he wants to take Eric somewhere familiar, somewhere he'd feel safe. That's what Reagan would do, if she were a wolf.

(She *is* a wolf. But there's no time to think about that now.)

Reagan's pedaling so hard that her lungs start to burn with all the air trapped inside her chest, but she doesn't stop, not to think, not to breathe, not until she hits Meadowbrook Lane.

It's near dark by the time she gets there. The street is deserted—all the children have long since gone inside, where it's light, where it's safe, and their mothers and fathers are there to watch over them. Reagan stashes her bike and helmet in the garage and stands, alone, staring across the street. She flips her black hoodie up and crosses the road, sneaking around the side of the house and slipping into the backyard.

She can't use the sliding glass door—too obvious—but one of the upstairs windows is half open. Without a ladder, there's only one way: Reagan scrabbles up the oak tree whose twisted limbs snarl close enough to nearly scratch the paint off the house.

It's not easy—wolves aren't natural climbers. Her sneakers slide against the bark, and she bites her tongue to keep from screaming as she almost falls from a tree branch that's barely strong enough to hold her weight. She hastily clambers over to the roof overhang, banging her knee against the shingles, and crawls across to the window, pushing up the glass pane and ripping apart the mesh screen with ease. Her nails are long and curled and so much sharper than they ought to be.

She sticks her head through the window to look inside, and her cell phone buzzes, startling her. She takes a breath, pulling back, and digs it out of her pocket. Mom. [Just checking in baby sry couldnt get night off luv u maybe bowling tomorrow?]

Reagan swallows against the tightness in her throat and blinks as everything in her vision turns blurry and wet. She doesn't want to think about tomorrow. She isn't sure there will *be* a tomorrow.

He's going to catch me. He's going to kill me. He's going to KILL ME—

[Sounds good,] Reagan texts back. [Love you, Mom.]

She scrubs at her eyes, turns off her phone, and slides into the house.

The bedroom is dark and smells like wet dog. The mattress is stained with ugly things. There is a small television and a VCR and a stack of tapes with boys' names written on the side.

Reagan gets down on all fours, carefully opens the door, and crawls out of the room.

The hallway is dark, and there are voices coming from downstairs—a whispered name, a woman screaming. It's the television, she realizes, but there are real voices too, murmuring beneath it, Eric's and the wolf's. She follows the sound down the hallway, going slow to avoid the floor creaking beneath her knees. She keeps low to the ground and makes her way to the staircase.

"I don't think that's—I mean, maybe I shouldn't—"

"Shhh," the wolf says.

Reagan peers down through the balustrade. Eric and the wolf are sitting on the couch, watching TV. The wolf is sitting too close to Eric. Eric isn't wearing his glasses, or his shirt.

There's an open bottle on the coffee table. Even from the stairs, Reagan can smell it, pungent and overwhelming. She shouldn't be able to nearly taste it, but she can.

"It's fine," the wolf says. "Your parents are out of town; they'll never know. And it's good, right? You like it, don't you?"

Eric nods but when he drinks from the bottle his whole face squishes tight and his eyes close. He sets it back down on the table too hard—the sound startles him and Reagan both. "Sorry," Eric murmurs, listing to the side.

It took Reagan too long to get to the house. Who knows how much Eric has already had to drink, or what the wolf might already have done. Wolves like to play with their food, and she has an idea what kind of game this wolf likes.

The wolf smiles and steadies Eric with one hand to the

chest. Reagan turns away as his fingers slide lower. "No apologies," the wolf says, his voice gritty with want and unspoken things. "We're having fun tonight, aren't we?"

"Yeah?" Eric doesn't sound very sure that's what's happening, but the wolf ignores him.

"Hey, are you getting hungry? I know I am."

Reagan's throat tightens and she forces herself to turn back.

"Yeah," Eric says. "Sure."

"Great. I'll order a pizza. You stay right there." The wolf touches Eric again, pushing him lightly backwards into the couch, and gets up, walking towards the kitchen.

Reagan waits until he's past and then crawls down the stairs and across the living room carpet, all the way to Eric's feet. His eyes are closed, and he doesn't hear her, not until she touches his knee; then he springs up fast, too fast. His head isn't ready for it. He collapses back down to the couch, blinking hard. She puts a finger to his lips.

They're as soft as she imagined and slightly damp too.

Reagan stands up and grabs Eric's hand, pulling him to his feet and frantically looking around. She'd been so focused on catching up that she never bothered to think of an escape plan. The sliding glass door is close but easily seen from the kitchen. If they can get to the front door, though, if she can push him and out and tell him to run...

"You think I couldn't smell you, little lady, the very second you crept into my home?"

Reagan spins and drops into a crouch instinctively. Eric stumbles behind her, falling back on the couch. The wolf walks into the room and leans casually against a wall—but too casually. He isn't as calm as he looks—his pulse is pounding, under his skin, and his eyes dart this way and that. Sweat pools under his armpits. He doesn't know what she wants, and he isn't sure what to do next.

That makes two of them.

"What's going on?" Eric asks. Reagan can smell the sweat on him, too—different, better, *human*. "Reagan? Mr. Garraty? What's—"

"You can't have him," Reagan tells the wolf. "He's not yours to have."

The wolf grins. "I didn't smell anyone's mark on him."

She bares her teeth. "Smell again."

The wolf takes a step away from the wall and Reagan growls, ready to spring if necessary. She won't win. He's bigger and probably faster, and in her haste, she forgot to grab any rocks or even a knife to slit the wolf's throat. If she attacks him now, he'll kill her—maybe even eat her, although she isn't entirely sure about that. She doesn't know if wolves are cannibals. That never came up in any of her research for the animal report.

"My," the wolf says. "Such lovely teeth you have, such big teeth. I didn't think you even knew what you were yet."

"I know," Reagan says, fighting to keep the bitterness and fear from her voice. "I know. And Eric's mine. Find another."

"I'm afraid you're mistaken," the wolf says. He's moving to the left now, circling her. "I've spent an awful lot of time on this one, becoming his friend, his mentor, the father he wishes he could have. His dad is out of town so often, you see. Eric needs a good strong male influence in his life."

Eric's breath stutters out and then starts up again, unsteady and too fast. He uses her back to push himself up. His fingers are hot through her sweater, like they're pressing into her bare skin. She growls again, involuntarily. She wants to turn around and drag him to the ground, push her body into his, bite into his neck.

"I think I wanna go home," Eric says, bumping the end table as he backs up. "Reagan? Can we—"

"Another step," the wolf says, "and I'll rip out your throat."

Eric stops.

"I told you," Reagan says. "He's mine."

"And how do you propose to keep him?"

She hesitates, almost a second too long. The wolf steps towards her—

"I'll tell," Reagan says, and the wolf stops.

"You'll *tell*?" the wolf asks incredulously.

Reagan nods. "If you eat Eric, if you so much as touch him, I'll tell everyone what I saw. And you can't kill me, either, you know. People…people know where I am. My mom knows. I texted her just before I crawled through your window."

"Then I'll kill her too," the wolf says.

Reagan's breath catches. She forces herself to inhale and exhale normally.

"That's a lot of bodies," she says, trying to shake the images of red and ripped flesh from her mind. "Or a lot of disappearances, anyway. You think they won't lead back to you?"

The wolf paces back and forth, watching. Reagan keeps her body between him and Eric. "You're bluffing," the wolf says finally. "I can smell your fear. You didn't tell your mom a thing."

Reagan's starting to regret that, but it's too late to go back now.

"I can smell you too," she reminds him. "Your shirt's stained with sweat. You're breathing too hard, and I can heart your heart thumping from here. You can't be sure I'm bluffing, can you?"

It's the wolf that growls this time, low and guttural. Hair stands on the back of Reagan's neck. He shifts his upper body weight forward and bends at the knees, all coiled up and ready to spring. "I could—"

"This is what we're going to do," Reagan says, straightening slowly and grabbing Eric's hand. "Eric is *mine*. He's coming with me. You can eat whoever you want, but not Eric, not my Mom, and not me." She turns to face Eric, takes in his pale skin and unfocused eyes. "Come on," she says, yanking on his hand.

But the wolf cuts in front of them, blocking their way to the door.

"No," the wolf says. "What's to stop you from calling the cops as soon as you leave? No, if you want this one… you'll have to eat him here."

Reagan stares at him and tries to cover her panic by laughing. It's not very convincing. She doesn't have a lot of practice at it. "Now you *want* me to eat him?"

"I want to know I can trust you," the wolf says. "I need to know you're a real wolf, not some pup with a guilty conscience. You'll eat him, and you'll do it now, or you won't leave this house alive."

He's left her no room to maneuver. She can't dart around him, can't jump over his shoulders, can't duck between his legs or push him aside. He's so much bigger than she'll ever be...but there has to be some other way, there *has* to be.

There's not.

Eric touches her shoulder hesitantly, gently pulling her back. "Reagan?" he asks, looking down at her, and that's a problem. He's too tall for what has to come next.

"I never wanted to do this," she whispers. "I hope you can believe that."

"Reagan, what's—"

She pushes him down hard, bringing him to his knees. He sways back, and she pulls him in, resting his forehead against her stomach. "If I promise you it's going to be okay, do you think you can believe me?"

"No?" Eric says. "I don't know? Are you...is this a sex thing? Or is it..." He swallows. "Are you going to kill me?"

"I'm going to save you," Reagan says. "I swear I'm going to save you. Close your eyes, okay?"

There are tears on Eric's face. "I'm scared."

"I know." She pushes the hair away from his damp forehead. "I know. Close your eyes now."

He does.

Reagan opens her mouth and stretches it as wide as it

will go, then wider than that, and wider. Bones snap in her face. Her jawbone hangs low.

I'm so sorry, she thinks, and swallows Eric whole.

He goes down easy, gliding down her gullet and resting low and curled in the bottom of her belly. It should be uncomfortable, those long legs and arms of his, sluggishly trying to push their way out. But it doesn't hurt at all—she feels warm and full for the first time in…she doesn't know how long. She's been so hungry, so fucking hungry. She hadn't even known how hungry, until now.

She could feel like this whenever she wanted. She could feel…sated, happy, *full*…and no one could stop her. No one could starve her. No one could scare her, not ever again.

"You know," the wolf says. "For a minute there, I wasn't sure you'd do it."

Reagan looks at him. He's not smiling—and why would he; she just ate his dinner—but she can see the relief in his eyes, hear his heartbeat start to slow in his chest. There's something else too, in the way he shakes his head. A faint… nostalgia, perhaps, like he can see a ghost of himself inside her. Like he can still taste that first little boy he swallowed, however many years ago.

Eric tastes like whiskey and saltwater and something else, something she doesn't have a name for. She wants to keep him. Her body is heavy, and all she wants to do is curl up and sleep with him trapped inside.

But she promised Eric she would save him, and she promised herself she wouldn't be this thing.

The wolf turns his back to her, heading for the front door.

"I think it's time for you to go, little lady. Not that it hasn't been fun, but—"

Reagan springs onto the wolf's back.

He staggers, falls forward. He's still bigger, but he's also off-balance, and she's heavier than she was ten minutes ago with the weight of Eric inside her. The wolf's nose smashes straight into the wall. Bones crunch and blood bursts, and he shrieks.

She wraps her legs around his waist and her arms around his neck and bites into the side of his throat as hard as she can. He yells out again and staggers backwards, slamming her into the wall. Reagan's head connects once, twice, three times; everything starts to tilt sideways and she can't catch her breath, but she laughs through the dizziness and a mouthful of blood. She squeezes tighter, tighter, tighter.

The wolf finally collapses to his knees. Blood gushes from his nose and spurts from his neck, and he blindly lashes out as she rolls off of him. His claws find her left arm and rake down her flesh. She dodges the next strike and circles around him, landing her heel into his ruined mess of a nose. He crumples, landing on his back, and she drops to straddle his waist and bare her teeth.

"Wait," the wolf says. "Please. Wait—"

Reagan grins and rips out his throat.

She chews her food well, long after the wolf has gone cold. Then she rolls onto her back and tries to lie still, tries to breathe and think through the frenzy. Her jawbone is almost touching her chest. She slams it back into place with the palm of her hand.

She needs to get the stones. It won't be finished until she fills the wolf's belly with rock, but Eric is still inside her, and she promised to get him out.

Reagan crawls to the kitchen and opens drawers until she finds the knives. She picks the biggest one she sees and rolls up her shirt. The edge of the blade is cold against her skin and she shudders. She takes a few deep breaths, readying herself…and then a hand squeezes her shoulder.

Reagan yelps and whirls around, clutching the cleaver, but it's not the wolf. The hunter stands in front of her, wearing his black hood and black half-mask, looking no different than he had four years ago.

"You came," she says. "You actually came."

"Late," he says. "Sorry. Looks like you've been doing okay, though."

He's not joking, which means his definition of 'okay' is hugely suspect, but she doesn't argue with him. Instead, she sinks silently down to the kitchen tile at his feet, lies back, and closes her eyes. She's been trying to forget since she was eleven, but monsters don't get to be wonderful and strange. Monsters get to die, and that's all.

The hunter squeezes her hand once, and then the agony comes.

Reagan tries not to scream, biting into her lower lip, maybe chewing it straight off while trying to hold the pain in. It doesn't work—she still screams for all she's worth, only getting control over her voice when the weight in her belly disappears.

She opens her eyes. The hunter is helping Eric out of her

stomach; he slides on the bloody tile, dripping and staggering and pale, but he's alive. He's *alive*.

"I'm so sorry," Reagan whispers.

Eric doesn't say anything.

She looks back at the hunter, who's watching her. "I'm ready," she says, and it's a lie because she isn't ready. She isn't ready at all. She's going to miss her mom and Eric and the sun and cartoons and history class and her future and all sorts of things.

"Are you sure?"

Reagan nods and stares up at the ceiling. Her stomach still burns, but not like it should—a human girl would be dying or dead right now, but blades alone can't kill a wolf. She thinks, given enough time, all the pain would melt away. Even her split skin might eventually stitch itself back together. Her insides want to heal. She can feel them trying.

They won't get the chance.

The hunter crouches next to her. "Okay," he says, and something sharp bites into her flesh, slides through and pulls away. Reagan glances down, confused. There are no rocks inside the hunter's hand, just a needle and thread. "But—"

"I only kill bad wolves," the hunter says. "Never the good ones."

"There are *good ones*?"

The hunter smiles softly as he sews. "It's not what you are that makes you a monster, little girl. It's what you *do*. That's the difference." He makes quick work of his stitches and soon she's in one piece again. The pain is not gone but significantly diminished. He offers her his hand.

She doesn't take it.

"You don't know," Reagan says. "The things I think about sometimes, the way I get. You don't know, how I get so..."

The hunter takes hold of her chin and forces her to look at him. "The trick isn't to stop wanting," he says. "Everybody wants."

"Then what's the trick?"

"It's..." The hunter looks around the room and shakes his head at whatever he sees. "It's finding someone who wants what you want, and when you want it. Then, *then* you can have your fill."

"Do you have what you want?" Reagan asks.

The hunter picks up his axe, still dripping with her blood, and smiles as he slides it back in the sheath with its sister. "I'm getting it tonight," he says. He offers her his hand again.

She still doesn't take it.

"You know," she says. "When you get back to writing your blog, it might not be a bad idea, talking about good wolves. *Some* people might find that kind of thing relevant."

The hunter inclines his head.

Reagan finally takes his hand and climbs to her feet. Eric, beside her, is silent and shaking. "Are you okay?"

Eric laughs.

Reagan bites her mess of a lower lip. "If there had been any other way..."

"But there wasn't," Eric says. "Right? You saved me?"

"She did," the hunter says.

"Mr. Garraty...he was going to eat me?"

"He was. And I doubt he'd have been kind enough to let you back out."

"But he's dead," Eric says. "You killed him, right?"

"She did," the hunter says. "But I'm here to make sure he stays that way. You two should probably go on home. Don't tell anyone you were here."

"What about the cops?" Reagan asks. "Fingerprints?"

"I'll take care of that," the hunter says.

They walk through the living room, stepping carefully around the wolf's body. Reagan stops when she reaches the front door and turns back to the hunter.

"I never thought I'd see you again," she says. "Thanks for coming back."

The hunter nods. He lifts his hand, and she thinks he's maybe going to pull her in for a hug, but instead he pushes his fingers against her bloody mouth, gently forcing her lips apart. "Look at these teeth of yours," he says.

She winces. "They keep growing."

"They're beautiful," the hunter tells her. "Don't be ashamed of them. You just keep using them well."

He releases her mouth and opens the door.

"Or," the hunter says. "You *will* see me again."

Reagan takes Eric back to her home.

He's still a little drunk and definitely in shock, so she gets him some water and tells him about wolves. She knows more than she did yesterday, a lot more, and most of it good. She saved Eric tonight. She couldn't have done that, if she was human.

She still cleans up, though, in the downstairs bathroom while Eric takes a shower upstairs. Her stitches are already fading and her jaw is firmly in place. Good. Mom probably couldn't handle seeing something like that.

Reagan's cutting two slices of birthday cake when Eric calls her name. She finds him sitting on the couch, looking out the window. He's staring at the wolf's house, which happens to be on fire.

Reagan has to pull her eyes away. "Cake?"

Eric turns. "Sure."

She sits down next to him. He takes her hand. "Thanks," he says.

"You're welcome."

They eat their cake in silence. They watch the house burn.

———————————————

FORWARD, VICTORIA

T IME MEANS LESS when you're dead, and you've been dead a long while[1]. Someone always brings you back, though. This go-around, it's two little girls with a Ouija board, playing at your grave. *Victoria Waite, Victoria Waite, kill my parents so I can stay up late!* The rhyme has changed again, it seems. It doesn't matter. Evolution is part of being a monster; the legend shifts, and you shift to fulfill it. They invoked your name. They're at a Significant Place. They wished for a death.

You wake.

You didn't wear the prom dress, that first time you resurrected.

It's part of your signature, red dress, no shoes, but it

---

1. violence, murder, parental abuse of children, child murder, religious abuse, bullying, blood/gore.

only happened...the second resurrection? The third? It doesn't matter, really. The legend shifted, so.

But that first time...you wore what your parents had buried you in: an ugly burlap sack of a nightgown, stained with your blood and sweat, piss and tears. The Redemption Gown, they called it. They never washed it, ever.

They hadn't meant to kill you. Arguably, they'd been trying to save you; they'd been trying your whole life, in secret, in the dark. Things went too far. Head cracked against a wall. Not breathing, for a moment. Confusion, panic. Disposal.

But you were still alive, a little, when they threw your body in the old well.

You don't remember the exact moment you died. You don't quite remember being dead. But you do remember waking up that first time: the tiny metal *thunk* of a penny hitting your cheek. A boy's voice—Todd's Clarke's voice—echoing through the well.

Victoria Waite, Victoria Waite.

Todd. Strawberry hair, big goofy smile. Earnest questions and silly little rhymes. His rented black tux had been a bit too big. You'd put your hands under his shirt. He'd laughed into your mouth.

Victoria Waite, Victoria Waite. Where did you go? Come back, it's late.

One thing you don't have is a signature weapon.

Of course, anything can be a weapon. You decapitated a

vice principal once with an office door. You electrocuted a mayor with gin and a string of Christmas lights. You don't exactly make puns—you never speak at all—but you've been known to indulge in the occasional irony kill. Your high school gym teacher, for instance. Shoving that golf club down his throat. Really, it made it further than even you would've imagined.

Still. You were all bird bones, back when you were alive, easily dislocated, easily crushed. Being dead is different: still skinny, forever sixteen and gawky, but there's *strength* in your arms and legs now, even though they're all bent and broken from the fall. It's a very particular type of strength, the kind you only get from climbing out of your grave.

You don't have a signature weapon because you don't want a signature weapon. Weapons break, get stuck. Weapons are less effective the more you use them. You've always preferred a signature method: making flesh origami with your own hands. Snapping bones, contorting bodies. Creating new, agonized shapes.

This is how you killed Molly's mom.

As a kid, Molly Guzman was an asshole. She shoved younger kids around. She stole their lunch money. She started that stupid chant. *Wait, Victoria Waite!* Which was inevitable, really, considering your surname—but still. You hated her guts. You hated her stupid pretty face. You hated her streak of pink hair and the bruises she didn't bother to hide and how she was too cool to know the answer, even though she obviously *did* know all the answers. You hated everything about Molly until you were fourteen, and she pushed you into the bathroom wall, and you kissed her, suddenly you just *had* to kiss her, and she kissed you back, she kissed you back *a lot*, and you were staring at each other, breathing hard, all what the fuck, what the *fuck*.

"This can't happen again," Molly said, and you agreed because if your parents ever found out—

No. They couldn't. They wouldn't. (They didn't.)

You kept your word; Molly did, too. The closet was almost the only thing you had in common, anyway. She was a poster child for juvenile delinquency; you were a B-student, trying desperately to become invisible. You never did become friends, exactly, but you...looked at each other often. Opposite ends of the hall, across the cafeteria. Nodded, occasionally, when no one else was looking. It was acknowledgement, validation. A silent confirmation: I see you. You see me. We're both still here.

You turned fifteen. You lost another battle with the guidance counselor, rushed off to what would surely be your new personal hell: Drama. You literally ran into Todd Clarke, *the* Todd Clarke. He'd laughed, kindly. Steadied you by the shoulders. Made up one of his dumb little rhymes.

Victoria Waite, Victoria Waite. Don't run so fast. For you, we'll wait.

Todd made you feel wanted, special. Like you deserved to be seen by the whole world.

Todd and Molly were seventeen when they staggered away from the bloodbath at the sheriff's station. They hadn't understood yet, that you weren't coming for them.

First, you came for your parents. But they had moved away by then. Nobody had stopped them; you were just a runaway, after all. No one in danger, no one who wanted to be found.

Then you came for the guidance counselor, but you found Todd's father instead. He was every gym teacher in every movie. He wore stupid shorts and bellowed inspirational speeches from sports films and could only be proud of his son, the baseball player. Todd, the short stop, had value. Todd, the theater nerd, was an embarrassment.

Todd, the worried boyfriend, had said, "Dad, I think they're hurting her."

Mr. Clarke, the terrible teacher and terrible father and well-respected member of the local country club, had said, "Nonsense. They're good folk. Don't go making waves, son."

Todd found that golf club just where you left it. The Sheriff found Todd near catatonic. Again.

It's strange how many children are unhappy when you murder their parents.

The little girls with the Ouija board, for example. They made a wish, and you honored it, and now the redhead is clutching her knees to her chest and screaming, screaming, screaming. There are always kids who mourn their neglectful parents and abusive teachers and oh-so-kindly neighbors, the ones who offer lemonade but refuse to ask questions, to interfere. Children's grief doesn't touch you. You aren't here to empathize; that's not something monsters can do, even if you were inclined to. Besides, there's always someone who understands that they're better off today than yesterday. Someone who's grateful and terrified in equal measure.

You step over the remains of the dinner party, over four broken plates and wine glasses and bodies. The redhead is still screaming, but blonde pigtails just watches from the corner. Watches as you pull the carving fork out of her father's neck, watches as the blood spurts, as he shudders and goes still. Watches as you discard the carving fork for the bread knife. As you pick up an invitation for the 20-year class reunion that he'd obviously decided to skip.

The little blonde girl doesn't say anything to you, doesn't smile, doesn't cry, doesn't laugh. But you've seen children like her before. You recognize her.

She's going to be just fine.

The last real conversation you had with Molly, before you died the first time:

"Okay, I know this is random, I know we don't really talk, but Homecoming? Todd asked me to go, and I already found this amazing dress, but my parents...look, it's not important, it's just they're not...great. Like, I'm not saying it's anything, just I can't—I can't get ready there, I can't stash my dress there, and I'd go to Todd's, but Mr. Carter doesn't like me; he'd *definitely* tell my parents. And I know you're not even going to the dance, and we're not even really friends, but—"

"Ugh, Jesus, quit talking already," Molly had said, studying her dark nails, so carefully bored. "I get it, my mom sucks, too. You can owe me or whatever, don't make a whole thing."

At seventeen, Molly and Todd both got arrested on the same day, for public intoxication and homicide respectively. Todd had no alibi for his father's murder, and unfortunately, his nervous breakdown about his dead girlfriend crawl-climbing up the well hadn't exactly cemented his credibility as emotionally stable. Todd was shoved in the cell next to Molly, although the sheriff soon yanked him out again, like a sacrificial goat.

"Here!" the sheriff yelled, as you eviscerated the second deputy. His blood had splattered everywhere: up the ceiling, through the bars, across the snowy white owl stitched into Molly's black crop top. "He's who you want, right? Take him, just take him!"

You didn't take him. Todd wasn't in your way, and he wasn't an adult, besides. He hadn't failed anybody yet. Instead, you grabbed the sheriff and slammed him headfirst into the brick wall, five times in rapid succession. Skull flat and sopping red by the time you dropped him to the floor.

Todd backed up slow.

You tilted your head, silently watching, as he knelt down by the dead deputy and grabbed the gory ring of keys with pale, shaking fingers. He dropped the keys twice, as he unlocked Molly's cell; she didn't even move, still staring at you, eyes glazed over, pupils huge. She was still very, very drunk, had barely been on her feet when you first arrived, collapsed forward and half-hanging from the bars. There was blood spatter against her cheek, too.

Molly had sobered up, mostly, a few hours later, enough to run without needing Todd's guiding hands. Still, she just kept staring at you, silent and blank. When you burst through the window, pulling her mother back by the shoulders. When you yanked so hard, Mrs. Guzman's spine broke straight in half at the T6 vertebrae.

You walk to the high school in your red prom dress. That dress. Maybe it had been your second resurrection, after all. Todd and Molly had graduated by then, fled town with most of their graduating class. Already, the legend of you had shifted. *Victoria Waite, Victoria Waite. Killed because she stayed out late.* It's true, and it's not; no one remembers the details. It was Homecoming, not Prom. A white-and-black dress, not red. Everyone forgets *why* you got caught—but of course, the rhyme scheme. It would have been ruined. *Victoria, the meek, Victoria, the fool. Killed for talking out of school.*

You're a monster. You adapt. You left the Redemption Gown behind.

You arrive at the high school now, find two women smoking in the parking lot, cheap carnival masks pushed up loosely atop their heads. You kill them quickly with the bread knife, serrated teeth to pale white throats. It takes longer to recognize the women as giggling girls from your algebra class. Their faces are sharper now, the dark circles obvious beneath their eyes. They've both grown so *old*. They're adults, and you can't help adults. They fail kids, break kids, kill kids. Adults deserve to die.

You drop the bread knife on the ground. Grab the closest beaded black mask. A masquerade reunion, all the better to elongate the suspense: who got pretty, who got bald, who got Botox, who got dead.

You slip the mask over your face and walk inside the gym.

It's a surprisingly packed event, considering how many coaches and teachers have died here over the years. People have grown too comfortable. It's been so long since you came back, and anyway, this isn't *your* class reunion because you didn't graduate with the class. There's one deputy on duty, at least; you corner him in the bathroom and break the white porcelain with his skull. There's a drunk man in a jester's mask who might have been on the baseball team with Todd. He slurs about how his teenage daughter is growing up nice, if you know what he means. You do know what he means. You break him at the knees and hips and elbows and shoulders until you can fold his body into the smallest locker, a collapsible corpse.

You return to the gym proper and immediately feel someone's eyes on you. She's standing across the way, wearing ripped black jeans and a glittery black top and a snowy white owl mask that covers everything but full black lips and the round shape of her jaw.

She nods at you. You stare back.

Someone starts screaming.

Ah. A body has been found.

Now everyone starts screaming. Running, hyperventilating, not knowing where to go. In her panic, a blonde woman bumps straight into you; you grab her by the hair as she starts to beg for herself and her children. "Please, my boys need me, you don't want them to live without a mother." She must be somebody's wife. Anyone from around here would know better.

There are rafters far above your head, painted in your school colors. If you launched her up, headfirst into one—

"Victoria!"

You drop the woman. She runs for her life. You barely notice. That voice—

You turn.

Todd Clarke stands ten feet away, taller, wider, unsmiling. His hair is still more strawberry than gray. The absolute love of your life—

And so old, old, old.

Your parents were only the first people to kill you. Todd was the second.

You killed Molly's mom. She deserved it. It was an open secret, just how much she deserved it—but still, no one wanted to make a scene. Not my monkey, not my problem. You killed Molly's neighbors next, and the last living deputy who tried to protect them. Then it was finally the guidance counselor's turn, who ran and ran from you. You couldn't run anymore, couldn't rush from place to place, but then, you didn't need to. You just kept following, one step at a time. His strength would give out eventually.

It did. At the well.

"I didn't know!" he screamed, begging, on his knees. "I didn't know what they'd do!"

But he should have. You lifted him in the air and strangled him with one hand. His tongue bulged. His face turned purple. It took him a surprisingly long time to die. You watched, dispassionately, and threw him to the side when it was over.

A boy started crying behind you. "Vic."

Todd, your Todd. You stepped toward him.

He scrambled backwards, hands up. "Wait, Victoria, wait!" he said, and you—

Stop.

It's surprise, more than anything, that stopped you. That old elementary school joke. Todd hadn't meant to say it; you could tell by how his hands covered his mouth, by the way he laughed hysterically through his fingers, by the sob tearing through his throat. Todd had never laughed like that before. Someone had hurt him. You needed to hurt them.

But he never gave you the opportunity.

"I'm sorry, Victoria," Todd said, and pushed you back down the well.

Todd isn't wearing a mask, only blue jeans and a soft sweater. He has a beard now. Glasses. He's holding a gasoline can in his hand.

"I hoped I'd never see you again," Todd says, "but I guess I knew I would."

You stare at him.

"Did you know I became a school counselor because of you?"

You didn't know. You step forward.

He smiles. Nothing like his old goofy smiles; this one is thin, weary. There's a woman's voice, somewhere behind you: "Fucking Christ, Todd, don't do this! She isn't after you—"

You recognize that voice, even after all these years. Todd knows it, too, but ignores her.

"I had to make sure," he says. "I couldn't stand by and see the system fail another kid, like you were failed. Like I failed you. I should've done something more. When Dad didn't help, I should've told someone else, I should've *made* you tell me what was really going on. I'm sorry, Vic. I'm still so sorry."

But you never blamed him, not back then. He was just a kid.

You step forward.

"This is the only way I can save you," Todd says. "It's the only way either of us will ever get peace. Don't we finally deserve that? Don't we deserve some fucking peace?"

You step forward. You step forward. You—

"Wait, Victoria Waite!"

Can't move.

Words are just words until they have power; until someone has used them to beat back the night. Those words are part of the legend now, and they always work, at least for a while. Others prefer to slow you down with rudimentary child psychology and a splash of theater, dressing up as your mother or father to scare you back. People rarely plan past that, though. They waste their precious few seconds. They hesitate. They die.

Todd doesn't hesitate. He reaches out and triggers a booby trap that explodes one of the ceiling rafters. It drops straight down, pinning you to the floor. Then he quickly sets the gym on fire, grabbing Molly—because of course it's Molly—and dragging her out as she kicks and bites back. He looks at you once, only once. He might be crying.

He leaves you to burn.

The last real conversation you had with Todd, before you died the first time:

"You'll be okay, right?"

You shrugged uncomfortably, trying to smile. The dance was perfect, nearly, anyway: kissing Todd, slow-dancing, how cute you felt in your feathered dress. "Like a snowy fucking owl," Molly had muttered a few hours ago, "so goddamn precious." Then she did your makeup while completely and aggressively ignoring you.

It was the best night you'd had in a long time, in forever. You didn't want to ruin that by talking about your parents: about the Redemption Gown, the punishments, how everything they did was because they loved you. Todd suspected something, had been trying to bring it up for weeks. You even overhead him telling his dad—who'd brushed it off, predictably. Not a surprise; it shouldn't have hurt. Your parents were influential. This was a secret-secret.

You tried sometimes, though. With Todd, who knew some of it and loved you anyway. With Molly, who didn't like you but might've at least understood. Just yesterday morning, you had a whole little breakdown in the guidance counselor's office when he said, "Your parents are so involved with the community; it must feel good, having that kind of support," and you...just ...*snapped*. Then you'd had to spend the next ten minutes doing damage control, all "I was just joking" and "I didn't mean 'hurt' *literally*" and "of course, everything is fine" before, thank God, you finally convinced him not to do something terrible, like call your parents.

You *did* want to tell someone. You felt like glass, most days, vibrating at some terrible frequency no one else could hear. Like you were gonna crack under the pressure, eventually; like if you didn't scream soon, you'd shatter— and maybe take out everyone in your vicinity, too: your parents, your teachers, Molly, Todd, all impaled in a storm of your broken, bloody shards. Sometimes, only sometimes, you thought maybe that would be better, maybe it would be a *relief*.

But mostly, you were determined to hold on. You

shouldn't tell anyone; you shouldn't *need* to. In two years, you'd graduate. In two years, you'd escape this place, and maybe it hurt, maybe sometimes it hurt so fucking much— but all you had to do was hold on a little longer.

All you had to do was survive.

Your hair is on fire. You red dress is on fire. Probably your flesh, too, although you can't actually feel it. That's what dying means: you can't feel anything anymore. It's the very best thing about being dead.

If you could still feel, that rafter would be too heavy.

If you could still feel, those flames would be too hot.

If you could still feel, you'd never survive the gym exploding around you.

But you can't. So you do.

You step outside. The parking lot is nearly empty now, only Molly, staring at the owl mask in her hands, and Todd, watching the gym burn down. Todd is close: to the fire, to you. His eyes widen. His lips part. He stumbles backwards, hands up.

He's the love of your life. But you can't feel that anymore, either. Love means less when you're dead, and you've been dead a long, long while.

"Wait," Todd says, "Victoria Waite!"

But that's the thing about weapons: they're less effective each time you use them.

"Wait," he tries again, desperately—

You snap Todd's neck so hard, he dies looking over his own shoulder.

"I'll save you," he'd murmured, as you slow-danced around the room, so softly you weren't sure if you were supposed to hear him at all. You pretended not to. You swallowed your scream. You never asked him for that. You never wanted to be *saved*.

The night had been perfect. You get it back on track, sneaking your hands under his shirt. He'd laughed into your mouth.

Molly stares at Todd's body.

She looks healthier as an adult: warm brown skin without any cuts or bruises, a thick, lovely waistline fed something besides French fries and vodka. Her hair is dark purple, buzzed next to nothing on one side. She's looking at Todd's body. She's looking at you.

"I still have your dress," Molly says. "I wanted to wear it tonight, poetic, or something. It was too fucking small."

You stare at her.

She smiles. It makes her look angry. "I tried to find your parents," she says. "Used to think if I could track those evil motherfuckers down, if you could finally just kill them... but I never could. Anyway, that's not what you want, is it? You wouldn't keep coming back if you wanted to sleep. I tried telling Todd that, that not everybody *wants* peace, but he couldn't…well. I guess we weren't really friends. Just people who survived together, for a while."

Molly's eyes are wet. The bigger she smiles, the angrier she looks. "Anyway," she says. "Here."

The owl mask is in one hand. A crumpled piece of paper is in the other. There are names written down. Addresses, occupations. Ages and sins.

You look up at her. She opens her mouth:

Victoria Waite, Victoria Waite. Send these fuckers to their fucking fates.

As a rhyme, it's not exactly elegant. And Molly is an adult. You can't help adults. Adults fail kids. Adults deserve to die.

But she isn't in your way. She invoked your name. She's at a Significant Place. She wished for a death.

Molly nods at you. You nod at Molly.

You slip the mask on, take the list. Walk away into the night.

ACKNOWLEDGMENTS

I never thought very seriously about putting together a short story collection. I daydreamed about it, occasionally, but it just seemed so unlikely to happen that I found myself focusing on other goals. Working on this project, however, has been an incredibly exciting experience for me. It's a bit like when I used to carefully create mix CDs for friends and family—only this time, I actually made all the music, and also, almost every song is full of dead things. I'm so very grateful to Merc Fenn Wolfmoor for giving me this amazing opportunity, and for being so generous, kind, and enthusiastic to work with. They have been an absolute delight.

I want to thank everyone at Clarion West, which I was fortunate enough to attend—God, ten years ago, now. It's hard to overstate how much of an impact CW has had on my life, and I know I wouldn't have this collection if I hadn't been a student there. Thank you to my classmates and friends: Brenta Blevins, Bryan Camp, Indrapramit Das, Sarah Dodd, M. Huw Evans, Laura Friis West, James G. Harper, Alyc Helms, James Herndon, Nik Houser, Henry Lien, Georgina Kamsika, Helen Marshall, Kim Neville, Cory Skerry, Greg West, and Blythe Woolston. You have all made me laugh. You have all made me a better writer. George, especially, thank you for just how many of these stories you've read and improved over the past decade.

Finally, thank you to all my friends and family who have supported me along the way. Mama, for always being here and always believing in me no matter what. Mekaela, for reading literally everything I've ever written in my life, for being my big sister and my absolute favorite person. You both mean the world to me.

ABOUT THE AUTHOR

Carlie St. George is a Clarion West graduate from Northern California who sleeps during the day, works at night, and thinks entirely too much about TV, fairy tales, and horror movies. Her short fiction has been previously published in Strange Horizons, Nightmare, and The Year's Best Dark Fantasy and Horror, among other anthologies and magazines. Find her chatting about writing, Star Trek, and other random nonsense on her blog mygeekblasphemy.com or at her Twitter @MyGeekBlasphemy.

ORIGINAL PUBLICATION INFO

"Some Kind of Blood-Soaked Future" originally appeared in *Nightmare* (October 2019).

"Three May Keep a Secret" originally appeared in *Strange Horizons* (November 2017).

"You Were Once Wild Here" originally appeared in *The Dark* (December 2019).

"Monsters Never Leave You" originally appeared in *Strange Horizons* (June 2020).

"15 Eulogies Scribbled Inside a Hello Kitty Notebook" originally appeared in *You Fed Us To The Roses* (October 2022).

"If We Survive The Night" originally appeared in *The Dark* (March 2017) .

"Every Day is the Full Moon" originally appeared in *Lightspeed* (December 2016).

"Spider Season, Fire Season" originally appeared in *Nightmare* (July 2020).

"Such Lovely Teeth, Such Big Teeth" originally appeared in *Strange Horizons* (March 2014).

"Forward, Victoria" originally appeared in *The Dark* (April 2021).

ALSO FROM ROBOT DINOSAUR PRESS

FLOTSAM BY R J THEODORE
A scrappy group of outsiders take a job to salvage some old ring from Peridot's gravity-caught garbage layer, and land squarely in the middle of a plot to take over (and possibly destroy) what's left of the already tormented planet.

THE WOLF AMONG THE WILD HUNT BY MERC FENN WOLFMOOR
When a knight mistakenly kills a corrupted nun, he has one chance to redeem himself. He must run with the Wild Hunt: an age-old trial of blood and courage, where every step hides peril and carnage. Few have ever returned from the fae-haunted land…for in the Wild Hunt, you run or you die.

ALSO FROM ROBOT DINOSAUR PRESS

THE MIDNIGHT GAMES: SIX STORIES ABOUT GAMES YOU PLAY ONCE ED. BY RHIANNON RASMUSSEN
An anthology featuring six frightening tales illustrated by Andrey Garin await you inside, with step by step instructions for those brave—or desperate—enough to play.

SANCTUARY BY ANDI C. BUCHANAN
Morgan's home is a sanctuary for ghosts. When it is threatened they must fight for the queer, neurodivergent found-family they love and the home they've created.

THEY DREAMED OF DEAD SHIPS BY BYRON M. KAIN
A terrifying plague sweeps the world, and there is nowhere safe...for it comes to you in a dream about a ship. And then it is too late.

A STARBOUND SOLSTICE BY JULIET KEMP
Celebrations, aliens, mistletoe, and a dangerous incident in the depths of mid-space. A sweet festive season space story with a touch of queer romance.

Find these great titles and more at your favorite ebook retailer!

Visit us at: www.robotdinosaurpress.com

CPSIA information can be obtained
at www.ICGtesting.com
Printed in the USA
BVHW071148091022
648971BV00002B/79

9 781949 936483